Praise for A Curse Awakened

"I adore the Weird Girls Series! I got pretty excited when I saw *A Cursed Awakened* took us back to before the girls moved to Tahoe, and we learn more about their curse. I really enjoyed it!" – **Christie's Love of Books**

"I definitely recommend this series for lovers of all things paranormal and awesome." - **USA Today, HEA**

"Cecy Robson is one of my favorite authors and I have yet to read a book by her that I didn't like. All the books in this series are written well with good world building. It's full of snarky humor, action packed scenes, strong and sexy heroes and kick ass heroines. You can also expect a heart break or two. If you like these things that I mentioned, this series is for you."
– **Under the Covers Book Blog**

"Robson proves once again that she is a master storyteller. . . Fans of the series will gobble this up and be eager to dive back in." - **Caffeinated Book Reviewer**

"I absolutely adore this series and the very fact that Ms. Robson gave us this much appreciated look into the sister's lives before the beginning of book one, is a huge testament to not only how wonderful a writer she is but what an awesome series this is. This is a must read for any fan. There is just so much more in this than you could have asked for or hoped for." –**My Guilty Obsession**

"*A Curse Awakened* is a thrilling and satisfying novella in the terrific Weird Girls Series. This is one of the best new Urban Fantasy series to hit the market in the last couple of years. It has everything you love in a good UF series. Great characters, plenty of paranormal creatures, originality, humor and romance. I can't recommend these books enough." **–Rainy Day Ramblings**

"Boasting an edgy, witty and modern style of storytelling, the reader will be drawn deep into this quirky paranormal world. Strong pacing, constant action and distinctive, appealing characters - including a gutsy heroine - will no doubt keep you invested."
- RT Book Reviews

"*A Curse Awakened* has everything I love about this series, strong and well-depicted characters, non-stop action, snarky humor, and a mix of rare legends and mythology. Cecy Robson's writing is excellent as always; she has a gift with words that easily captures the reader and traps him/her between the pages."
–The Bookaholic Cat

"Jam packed with action, suspense, kickass girls, hot guys, humor and all out weird girls, this series has me coming back for more and more."
- Night Owl Reviews (Top Pick)

"This series has everything paranormal romance and urban fantasy lovers could possibly want. From Action, to danger, to steamy hot romances, to strong characters and bonds, plus a bit of mystery and politics, what's not to love? I'm

only sorry it took me this long to find this series…But now all I want is more and will be anxiously waiting until I can get my next Weird Girls fix."
- A Book Obsession

"If you're a fan of urban fantasy or paranormal romance and you're NOT already reading this series… START!... From start to finish, Ms. Robson's writing is crystal clear and concise yet beautifully descriptive and YES, she can write the romance parts AND the fight scenes equally well. Hence why I have no reservations about recommending this series to just about everyone I know. " **- My Para Hangover**

"A Curse Awakened is everything that a prequel novella should be. All those pesky questions about Celia and her sisters' curse are answered. Where is came from, why and of course how they got their full powers."
–The Reading Cave

"Okay, its official! Cecy Robson is one of the grand dames of cliffhanger finishes and she does it with like two sentences. She layers a shock on top of a shock so that I just sit there staring at the last page with a whimpering 'no, it can't end there' on my lips before hoping like mad that the next book is coming out some time this year or praying for strength if the release date is more than a year off...Urban Fantasy fans get busy and grab this series up. Paranormal Romance fans, you won't be disappointed either." **- Delighted Reader**

BY CECY ROBSON

The Weird Girls Series

Gone Hunting
A Curse Awakened: *A Novella*
The Weird Girls: *A Novella*
Sealed with a Curse
A Cursed Embrace
Of Flame and Promise
A Cursed Moon: *A Novella*
Cursed by Destiny
A Cursed Bloodline
A Curse Unbroken
Of Flame and Light
Of Flame and Fate
Of Flame and Fury (coming soon)

The Shattered Past Series

Once Perfect
Once Loved
Once Pure

The O'Brien Family Novels
Once Kissed
Let Me
Crave Me
Feel Me
Save Me

The Carolina Beach Novels
Inseverable
Eternal
Infinite

APPS

Find Cecy on *Hooked – Chat stories APP* writing as Rosalina San Tiago
Coming soon: *Crazy Maple's Chapters: Interactive Stories APP:* The Shattered Past and Weird Girls Series

A Curse Awakened

A WEIRD GIRLS NOVELLA

CECY ROBSON

The night I was born, a bat swept down in front of my father as he ran along a cobblestone road. My father ignored the bat in his haste to reach the Central American hospital where my mother labored with me. The bat disappeared in the shadows. In its place emerged a man, his dark skin bare, his voice ominous, his imposing form blocking my father's path. "Be wary of this one," he warned in Spanish. "She's not like the others."

Okay, I'll confess. This didn't happen. But it sounds way cooler than simply admitting my father used to kiss me goodnight wearing vampire fangs, and that he was the first person to trigger my overactive imagination.

I've always loved telling stories and getting a laugh. I've also enjoyed hearing stories, especially of the paranormal variety. Being of Latin descent, I heard many tales of spirits who haunt the night, of death lurking in the darkness waiting to claim her victims, and of circumstances which could only be explained by magic and creatures not of this earth.

The stories frightened me. I often slept clutching a crucifix while my plastic glow-in-the-dark Virgin Mary stood guard on my nightstand. And still I begged for more.

Sometimes the beasties of the night bumped too hard, and I swear I could see ghosts floating above me. I trekked on despite my fear, surviving each night while my plastic protector looked on.

On May 1, 2009, I decided to write a story about four unique women who must trek through their own darkness where supernasties bump hard, and bite harder. *The Weird Girls* series is the journey of Celia, Taran, Shayna, and Emme Wird, sisters who obtained their powers as a result of a backfired curse placed upon their Latina mother for marrying outside her race. Their story begins when the supernatural community of Lake Tahoe becomes aware of who they are, and what they can do.

"Weird" isn't welcomed among humans, nor is it embraced by those who hunt with fangs and claws, who cast magic in lethal blows, and who feast on others to survive. I wanted to show "weird" could be strong, brave, funny, and beautiful.

My "weird" girls will often face great terror, just like my seven-year-old frightened self, except without a glow-in-the-dark icon to keep them safe. Despite their fears, they fight like their lives depend on it, with only each other to rely on.

Sometimes, the darkness will devour the sisters. And sometimes, good won't succeed in kicking evil's ass. But just like glow-light Mary, there is hope. And there is humor—often twisted, a little inappropriate, and always hilarious—very much like a father saying goodnight to his children wearing a rubber ghoul mask and owning a collection of fake fangs no adult male should possess.

So, read on and check out my *Weird Girls* series. Maybe you'll find I'm really "not like the others."

Salud!

Cecy

ACKNOWLEDGMENTS

There are two people who I wouldn't be here without: my agent, Nicole Resciniti, and my husband, Jamie. Nicole works to make my writing dreams a reality. Jamie believed in me from the very first pages I typed. I'm so blessed to have them in my life.

.

Chapter One

There are many reasons a gal can expect a call from an ex-boyfriend—he misses said gal, still loves her, wants her back, can't live without her.

I heard: "Celia, you have to help me. Vampires want to eat me and my dad."

Welcome to my world.

I held the phone away from me for a second and stared at it like it was a killer bee about to sting, then returned the antiquated piece of black plastic to my ear. "Ah, Danny?"

It wasn't like I didn't know it was him. Even without my supernatural hearing, his shaky, terrified voice was as recognizable as his crazy steel-wool hair my sisters used to gape at. I debated whether to hang up. We were moving in a few days, leaving Jersey and all its memories behind to start new lives. Too much bad had happened to us here. It was time for something good. But I couldn't bring myself to hang up and disconnect him from my life. This was Danny. Without his academic help, I'd have flunked out of nursing school and my sisters would have ended up back in foster care.

"Celia, please help me."

I grimaced, knowing this would only lead to pain and torture, mainly mine. "Where are you?"

"In Warren, at my dad's. But it's not safe. Can I meet you somewhere near your place?"

My claws protruded as I tapped the old battered Formica counter. I withdrew them with a great deal of effort. "How long will it take you to get to that old soccer field three blocks from me?" I whispered.

"I can meet you there in twenty." He let out a breath. "Thanks, Celia."

I leaned on the doorframe separating the kitchen from our tiny family room. My younger sisters were rushing around the small space, boxing up everything we'd planned to donate to charity and oblivious to my conversation. "Don't thank me yet. I'm not making any promises." I returned the phone to the charger, keeping my sisters in my sights. Agreeing to meet him was my second mistake; the first was answering the damn phone.

Shayna scrunched her pixie face when she caught my hardening expression. She abandoned the box she was loading with old clothes and adjusted her sleek black ponytail. "Who was that? And why do you look so down, dude?"

"It was Danny."

Her grin lit up the dim room. "Danny Matagrano?" I nodded. "How's he doing?"

"Lousy. Vampires are trying to eat him."

Emme paused from folding a pair of old sheets, her hands lowering along with her slacking jaw. "How did he . . ." She swallowed hard and tried to speak clearly. "I-I thought those things mostly hung out in the bigger cities. Like New York."

I shrugged. "I guess they decided to check out Jersey. Either that or they came here specifically for him and his father. He wasn't clear. All he said was that he needed help."

Taran continued wrapping knickknacks in newspaper as if I hadn't spoken. Too bad her swearing under her breath gave away her exact thoughts. "Well, sucks to be him—literally. Send him some garlic, say a couple of Hail Marys on his behalf, and wish him well. This is so not our business. Vampires. *Freaking* vampires. This goddamn world is so messed up."

I tucked a strand of my long wavy hair behind my ear. "I told him I'd meet him at the old soccer field in twenty minutes. I can't just—"

Taran threw her box on the floor with enough force to crack the ceramic trinkets she'd wrapped. She stormed up to me and shoved her face in mine, her blue eyes ablaze with her hidden fire. If I were anyone else, she would have throat punched me. "Four days, Celia!" she yelled. "That's the time we have left in this state. Four days and we're outta here—new life, new jobs, new home. This is not the time to go looking for trouble!"

"I'm not looking for trouble!" I growled.

My tigress's eyes replaced my own. My vision sharpened—making everything and everyone clearer—an asset every predator needs to hunt its prey. Taran cringed, edging away from me, and so did my sisters. I lowered my gaze and breathed slowly, withdrawing my inner beast and soothing her as best I could. She didn't want to hurt my sisters, and neither did

I. But my anger was often the whip that riled her—and me—into a manic phase that searched for blood.

And the last time I let her loose, she got that chance to bite.

I opened my eyes when my breathing slowed and the blood racing through my veins ceased pounding against my eardrums. Embarrassed by my lack of control, I walked into the kitchen and stood near the glass door leading out to the large yard. My eyes scanned the well-groomed grass. I'd mowed it that morning while Emme saw to the pretty flower beds where we'd finally scattered our foster mother's ashes. Ana Lisa had loved her tiny house, and would've wanted us to stay. But Taran was right, it had been years since Ana Lisa lost her battle with cancer and now, it was time for us to move on.

Long skinny arms wrapped around my waist. Shayna was braver than her perky demeanor would ever reveal, but she also recognized that I'd reined in my beast. At five foot five she was two inches taller than both me and Taran, and exactly five inches taller than our Emme. She placed her chin on my shoulder. "You're getting stronger, Ceel," she whispered. "It didn't take you long to tame that kitty cat of yours."

Shayna meant well. But her optimistic attitude didn't adequately describe my state of being. "If that were true, she'd never come out to play without my permission." I turned to face them. "I—*we*—could never hurt you. I hope you know that. But sometimes, when she wants to break free, it is to do harm. Except there's no one around to send her after . . . at least not anymore." Not since I killed the men who'd killed our parents. We hadn't had much, but the gang members who'd broken into our home robbed us of our most precious asset—our beloved mother and father.

Taran huffed and squared her shoulders when my voice trailed and she caught traces of my guilt. "You need to get over that, Ceel. Those bastards deserved everything that beast of yours unleashed."

It was easy for Taran to say. She hadn't heard the men begging for their lives. She hadn't slashed their throats or watched them bleed, listening for their hearts to stop beating so she could finally walk away. Their voices stayed with me, screaming for mercy during my worst nightmares. And those nightmares were brought on by stress. So, between the strain of selling the house and our decision to become traveling nurses, my prey had visited me every night that month.

I shoved my feet into an old pair of sneakers by the sliding glass door, not wanting to dwell on those I couldn't bring back. "I'd better go meet Danny. He should be at the field soon."

Taran rolled her eyes and adjusted her tiny cropped shirt. "Fine, but not without us. The last thing I want is you straddling his skinny ass and making skinny-ass babies." She swore again since, well, that's how she rolled.

"I'm not straddling Danny," I insisted. "What we had was sweet, but it's very over." I grabbed the house keys and marched out with my sisters behind me. I held open the door, waiting for everyone to scamper out. As I jiggled the old lock to the door, Emme tugged on the edge of my wolf T-shirt I'd purchased on a recent trip to the Bronx Zoo. I had a soft spot for wolves.

"Um, Celia, you said what you and Danny had was 'sweet.'"

I continued to fiddle with the sticky lock, trying to pull the key out without breaking it. "That's right."

"Well, forgive me for being nosy, but didn't you and he . . ."

I withdrew the key, blushing a little, though it was probably hard for others to tell given my olive skin tone. Sex with Danny had consisted of awkward hand movements and one or two thrusts. Not exactly the stuff of bedroom legend. In all fairness, that was almost seven years ago, back when I was seventeen, he was nineteen, and neither of us had any experience. "We did, but it's not like it was love or anything."

Emme didn't seem to understand, mostly because she still had her heart set on happily-ever-afters. "Then why did you do it?"

"I thought it was time." I walked down the two little wooden steps. "It was a stupid reason, but I'm glad it was him. He was good to me. He was good to all of us."

I must have spoken loud enough for Taran and Shayna to hear. Taran knitted her dark brows, drawing attention to her startling blue eyes. "He was, until he dumped you when he left for Stanford. Damn it, Ceel. I'm still pissed at him for that. I mean, you were totally Bambi. Danny? Hell, he was a walking Bullwinkle at best."

I opened my mouth to argue, but Taran was sort of right. Danny was a lot of things: adorable, kind, and smart enough to get into Stanford for biochemistry. And it still hadn't been enough. He wasn't strong, physically or emotionally, not really. My weight topped out at a little over a hundred pounds, yet I could knock his lanky frame and a few linebackers on their asses. In Danny's defense, he didn't possess the inner beast I did. But maybe that was my problem. I was too "Hulk" and he was too human.

We crossed the street and walked into the small alleyway separating the neighborhoods. "I don't want you to be mad at him, Taran. He didn't break my heart," I said quietly. "He hurt my pride, but that's about it." I rubbed my arms, remembering the day we broke up. He cried while I stood there listening and trying to make sense of his actions. I'd thought he really liked me . . . and maybe that was the cause of his tears. "He was right, you know—about not being the guy I needed. I didn't understand then, but I do now."

"Then what kind of man do you think you'll end up with?" Emme asked softly.

Shayna and Taran slowed their steps, knowing Emme had hit a raw nerve. They all dated. Men rarely glanced in my direction. And if one did, he instinctively took several long steps back. Humans couldn't see my tigress, but they knew something dangerous lurked within me.

And they were right.

"I don't know if I'm meant for anyone, Emme."

Her fair and freckled face heated, despite the cooling air. "I think you are. But I also think you need to believe it's possible."

We crossed the next street, where a few kids played Wiffle ball. "Freaks," one of the more daring boys shouted, before running off at the sight of my glare.

"Eat shit, you little bastard!" Taran called after him. Her stare drifted to each of us. "I'm so tired of these punks and this damn state. I can't wait to get the hell out of here."

No kidding. As nurses we should've been in high demand, but children weren't the only ones who sensed we were different. If it hadn't been for our foster mother begging the director of the nursing department to let me into the program at the tender age of sixteen—and then practically blackmailing her former manager to hire me after I graduated two years later—I wouldn't have landed a decent job. Taran, Shayna, and Emme had an easier time because of their beauty and ability to portray gentler, more trusting sides. No matter how soft I tried to make my husky voice, or how professional I came across, humans could sense my inner monster, waiting for the chance to claw and nibble. Thankfully, our traveling-nurse jobs had only required phone interviews.

We crossed onto the small path that led into the old soccer field as swirls of orange and red painted the sky. Dusk at the end of September brought an almost immediate chill. My tigress kept me warm enough, but my sisters needed to button their sweaters.

My old canvas sneakers crunched the dry grass of the overgrown lot. This was once a well-kept soccer field, until the county could no longer afford to maintain it. A sign near the edge proclaimed the land sold. In another month, construction on a new townhouse complex would begin. Just what Jersey needed, more homes erupting over a tiny plot of land.

On the opposite side, a white Ford F-150 rolled to a stop over the cracked asphalt.

Danny cut the lights and motor. The encroaching darkness shadowed his face inside the truck's cab, but I still caught his lanky shoulders slumping with relief when saw me. Poor guy probably couldn't put on muscle if he tried. I smiled. I couldn't help it. Scrawny, awkward, or not, it was great to see the guy who'd been more than a boyfriend. He'd been an actual friend.

My grin widened. That's probably why I didn't nut-punch him when he dumped me.

We walked slowly toward him, until Danny threw open the driver's door and stumbled to the ground.

Shit.

From one blink to the next, I was kneeling beside him and pulling him into a sitting position. Blood dripped from a makeshift bandage wrapped around his knee.

"I'm okay," he choked out.

"No, you're not, Danny." My small fingers reached to gently touch the skin beneath the black frames of his thick glasses. I bit back a swear. Swollen purple skin reduced Danny's right eye to a mere slit and the scent of dried blood seeped from his nostrils. "Vampires?"

"Yeah. They weren't nice."

My sisters sprinted toward us. Emme and Shayna screamed over Taran's barrage of cursing, this time in Spanish. Taran pointed as more blood oozed from his leg. "Son of a bitch. Were you knifed?"

"No. They had claws." He looked at me. "Sort of like Celia's, only straighter. They could elongate them like their fangs."

Emme gasped. "Fangs?"

Shayna pried her eyes from Danny's injuries long enough to answer Emme. "Well, they are vampires, Em."

"Their fangs seem to be pointier," Danny added, putting pressure on his wound. "No offense, Celia."

"None taken." I motioned Emme closer when blood seeped between Danny's fingers. "Try to seal the wound."

She nodded and reached to hold his hand. "I won't be able to mend it completely, but I can try to stop the bleeding, okay?"

He nodded. With her small hand carefully covering his, her soft yellow light spread from her fingertips until it enclosed them both. Danny scrunched his face in agony, sweat dripping down his forehead.

"Does it hurt?" Emme asked.

"It burns . . . a little."

No, it burned a lot. Emme had tried to heal me once. *Once*. I'd cut my finger chopping lettuce and I could swear she was pouring acid on my hand. If not for my obvious need for stitches, I'd have taken my chances. She'd gained her power to heal and move objects when she reached puberty—the same time Taran and Shayna had acquired their powers. Cuts and bruises faded easily from Emme's skin pretty much from the moment she sustained them. All it took was a little concentration. It didn't hurt her to tend to her own injuries. But us? Let's just say she hadn't quite mastered her *touch*.

She kept her eyes closed as Danny squirmed beneath her. "Just a little more. I'm right at the bone."

Danny jumped so hard I practically caught him in my arms. Something snapped. "Oh, shit," Taran gasped. "Did she break his bone?"

Emme whipped back her hand, her skin blanching with fear. "Did I?"

I pulled the dressing off his leg. "No. The bandage ripped when he jerked." I used the clean side to wipe his thigh. Emme had sealed the wound. The skin appeared mangled but the bleeding had stopped. With time, hopefully the skin would smooth out. Hopefully.

I took in his state. Emme's efforts had also diminished the swelling to his eye. His injuries were barely noticeable now, but it didn't erase the fact that those vamps had pounded my poor defenseless friend. "Where's your dad?"

Danny bowed his head. "They took him—the vampires. He'd been acting funny on the phone over the last few months, but he'd grown worse. When he didn't return my calls last week, I thought maybe he was sick and not telling me, so I flew out from California." He removed his glasses and rubbed his eyes as if too tired to continue. "That was two nights ago. I found him pale, distraught, and acting bizarre. He kept saying the Mafia was after him and we needed to run."

"Son of a bitch." Taran stopped her agitated pacing. "*The* Mafia?"

Danny shook his head. "No. He mistook them for Mafia, but I think at best they're vamps with Mafia ties. There's this female among them that seems fixated on my father. I think she's been drinking from him. It's odd. She's odd. The whole thing is . . . *odd*."

Shayna grimaced. "You mean aside from her drinking blood?"

Danny tried to stand. "Yeah. I don't know if vampires can be mentally ill. From what I've researched so far, they're immune to diseases. But nothing I've read mentions anything about being immune to insanity."

I steadied him with my hand. "Why have you been reading up on vamps? I mean, I know since you've learned about us, you've been curious, but . . . I'm not a vampire."

He sighed, watching me with his dark sad eyes. "Believe it or not, I thought I could help you. You and your sisters have something special."

"Ah, no, we don't." Taran glared his way. "At best we're atom bombs ready to detonate." As if to make a point, a puff of blue and white smoke from her fire popped and sizzled above her head.

Danny returned the glasses to his face. "I don't agree. There're not a lot of books available here in the U.S. about the supernatural—the real kind, I mean—*weres,* witches, vamps, those types of beings. But I've purchased a few ancient volumes from old libraries in Europe, where most legends stem from actual truths. I haven't been able to find much about what you are or what you could be. In fact, I'm positive you're different from any race of humans or preternaturals on earth."

"Yay for us," Taran muttered.

Danny offered a sympathetic smile. "One thing I have learned a great deal about are curses and magic in general." His gaze skipped to each one of us. "I think you're all in a bind."

"No shit," Taran snapped. "I'm surprised we haven't killed each other."

Danny held out a hand. "No, that's not what I mean. I think you've been bound—in the magical sense. Sort of like a noose or tie that holds your powers back, and therefore your control." He focused on me. "Celia, I think you can manage your powers best because your tigress gives you added strength. Picture a pit bull on a leash. You're going to pull harder against it than another, smaller breed, making it harder to hold you back."

Shayna inched forward. "Um, Danny, maybe you should watch the dog references. *I* understand what you're trying to say, but Taran's a little touchier." She motioned to Taran with a jerk of her head. "Know what I mean, little guy?"

Taran narrowed her eyes, proving Shayna's point.

Danny's mouth popped open. "I'm sorry. I wasn't trying to insult you, ladies."

I barely heard his apologies, my ears honing in on the rumble of two motors. Two cars entered the dead-end street leading to the field and to us. The roar of their engines didn't sound familiar or appropriate for the area. We were in blue-collar territory and these vehicles were definitely not your standard beaters. And instead of slowing down when they entered the narrow street, they sped faster, like cheetahs who'd found a herd of wounded gazelles.

My tigress growled a warning. Taran's blue eyes blanched to white, her magic sensing another's approach.

Danny jerked around upon seeing the first car barrel up the small incline. "It's the vampires. *Run!*"

Chapter Two

Danny raced across the field. Emme followed. The rest of us remained, confusion and surprise cementing us in place. I'd never seen a vamp. Never smelled one, never heard one. And when Danny told me a few years back that they were real, I didn't find it too hard to believe. After all, if my sisters and I could exist, why couldn't other supernaturals exist, too?

That said, I was dumbstruck by their appearance. Taran, Shayna, and I gawked as *GQ* model types in black suits emerged from two souped-up red Porsches. There were seven, three from one car, four from the other. They removed their sunglasses. A blond who resembled an edgy James Dean grinned my way as the aroma of sex and chocolate overtook my senses. "Well, what do we have here?"

Shayna leaned closer to me. "Um. Why aren't they sparkling? Shouldn't they, like, *sparkle*?"

I don't think the so-called creatures of the night appreciated the reference. They hissed and stalked toward us. "Grab some wood," I muttered.

"Already got some," James Dean said, his eyes never leaving mine.

Okay. Direct eye contact from a male. That was a first. If I weren't already scared out of my mind, I might have also been skeeved by his comment. As it was, my beast licked her chops, perceiving his leer more as a challenge. I swore in my head, knowing she'd found him more appetizer than threat.

From the corner of my eye, I saw Shayna crouch and lift three broken sticks from the ground. As the sun set behind us, the last trickle of light traced along the lengthening sticks. Shayna transferred the metal from her gold necklace into the pieces of wood, morphing them into long, sharp needles. She clutched two tightly in one hand while twirling the other between the fingers of her opposite hand.

That gave the vamps their first "oh shit" pause. My protruding claws gave them their second. "What are they?" a dark-skinned vamp asked, his nails and his incisors protruding in response.

James Dean smirked. "Don't know. Don't care. But this one is mine."

I didn't see him move. All I felt were his hands at my throat. His thumb teased my jugular as his light eyes drilled into mine. "You won't scream. You won't fight," he commanded, hardening his voice. "You're just going to feel real good." He widened his mouth and drove his fangs toward my neck.

My claws punctured through the crotch of his designer pants and twisted as the point of a fang traced against my skin. A sound somewhere between a garbled choke and squeak tore through his throat. Another vamp yanked me by the hair, trying to wrench me off. I took James Dean with us, squeezing tighter.

"Rob," James Dean choked, sounding more little girl with a sore throat than vicious bloodsucker. *"No."*

The hold to my hair loosened. "Huh?"

I used Rob's hesitation to drive my free hand through his belly, digging through his torso while my right wrung Jimmy Dean's sausage—a crude and outrageous tactic perhaps, but considering the prick tried to bite me, I didn't care about being polite.

Taran screamed. Something smoked. And heat smacked against my face. I would've panicked if another vamp hadn't howled back in agony. Shayna's grunt followed another deep-throated hiss just as my claws felt the first beat of the vamp's heart. I thrust my hand up and was rewarded with a stream of warm ash, blinding me.

"She killed Rob!" someone roared.

James Dean wrenched from my loosening grip, wailing. I jerked up and swiped the ash from my face. Another vamp fell against me with two of Shayna's needles jutting from his sternum. He writhed against me, trying to pull them from his chest.

I did what any other tigress would've done in my place—I wrapped my legs around his waist and tried to yank his head from his shoulders.

And, well, didn't that piss him off.

He hissed, nailing me hard in the ribs with his elbows. I lost my breath with every impact. Panic and pain made me pull harder while my claws hacked into his neck. The last crunch of his vertebrae rang in my ears before a rain of ash streamed over my chest and shoulders. I heaved, spitting out the bits of vamp coating my tongue.

James Dean staggered back, clinging to his blood-soaked pants as he wrenched open his car door. He retreated, snarling, while his furious face took in the scene down in the field.

Blue and white flames encased Taran's form as she dashed after a vamp with one of Shayna's needles sticking out of his eye. She wasn't fast, but at that moment, neither was he. Shayna chased behind another vamp, who was already partially decapitated from the sword she'd transformed from a branch. Three vamps were re-dead. Two soon would be. The one who'd seen enough was hauling ass in his red Porsche. That left one more.

Too bad he was the biggest and baddest of all.

The other vamps had been more lean. This vamp was all muscle and had Emme and Danny cornered against an old oak at the far end of the field.

My legs pumped across the waist-high grass as he lifted Danny and Emme by their throats. Unlike "Rob," this guy wasn't dumb and he wasn't slow. He sensed my approach and dropped them, dipping his heavy body low as I leapt.

I collided into the ground several feet away. He kicked me in the gut before I could rise, making me flip. I rolled with the momentum and the stomach-lurching nausea burning its way up my throat.

My tigress eyes replaced my own and a snarl shook my chest.

"What the *fuck* are you?" He prowled forward, hissing with fury.

I caught his foot when he stomped it down toward my skull and rammed my heel between his legs. The agony searing my belly weakened the impact yet the thrust was enough to buy me time. Time to leap—okay, more like *stagger*—to my feet. He swung his meaty fist. I dropped into a deep crouch and propelled upward, nailing him in the jaw with an elbow.

The thing about learning to fight on the street is that it taught me to endure pain and go for the win at whatever the cost. That meant not being afraid to fight dirty. There was no grace or carefully choreographed jabs and sideswipes. It was blow after blow, knowing I couldn't stop, even if he went down. No mercy. No hesitation. That's what determined who'd win.

My fists and legs morphed into a flurry of windmills. Except it wasn't enough, no matter how hard I pummeled or how deep my claws raked his flesh.

The Goliath vamp cuffed me hard in the face, bashing my nose in and sending blood shooting out like a hose. It was the one hit he managed, but that's all he needed. I couldn't match him in strength. Not in my human form.

Maybe that's what my tigress finally needed to bust through the chain that bound her. A little motivation in the form of mind-numbing terror and teeth-rattling pain.

My body smacked onto the littered ground, covered in fur, three times as large, and madder than hell.

I spun, crouching on four legs, and pounced on the befuddled vamp. But just like I wanted to survive, so did he. My claws punctured his face, shredding it like weather-beaten cardboard as his nails pierced through my dense shoulders, trying to force me off. Our fangs snapped, our bodies slammed together, beating each other with everything that we had.

Taran and Shayna screamed, but not because of my brawl.

"Emme, no! Stop! You have to calm down," Taran screamed at her.

"*Don't*. She's okay. Ceel's okay!" Shayna yelled.

The vamp kicked me off him. And that was probably the only thing that saved me.

There was a rattle behind me, followed by the strong sense of impending death. I flattened out on my stomach as the remaining Porsche jetted across the field, mashing the vamp against a row of trees.

His body busted open, splattering bits of brain and bone across bark, dirt, and a cluster of overgrown blackberry bushes. Disturbing? Yes. Gag inducing? Uh-*huh*. But it was the remainder of his body crawling toward me that just didn't seem fair. Emme had hit him with a *car*. In any other *Buffy* episode, that would have been enough.

The claws of one hand dug into the earth. He only had half a body, and that half still advanced like a slow-moving crocodile, writhing in agony, yet determined to kill me. Without eyes to see and a brain to direct it, it catapulted toward me. I jerked from its path just a little too soon.

In an effort to "help," Shayna converted a twig into a stake. It sucked monkey snot that my sister's aim wasn't the greatest. A pathetic roar squeaked from my throat as her stake found my ass. My eyes rolled into my head as stabbing pain rocked my butt cheek.

"Dude. I am, like, *so* sorry!"

The vamp continued to crawl toward me. Punctured rear and all, I drove my paw into his exposed heart and squished. My vision spun from the feel of the rupturing vessel and the multitude of painful spasms rocking my body. But despite the throbbing, the feel of the warm ash erupting beneath my claws allowed me to take a breath. He was dead. And he could no longer hurt us.

I blinked my blinding tears away as my body *changed* back to my smaller half, tightening around Shayna's stake like an angry fist. "Get . . . it . . . *out.*"

I shrieked at Danny's first attempt. And his second. And his third. If it wasn't for the overwhelming scent of sex and chocolate returning, I may have slapped him senseless.

A dark boot stepped into my line of vision. Another vampire had arrived.

Chapter Three

Waist-length ebony hair drifted in the small breeze, falling into a perfect cascade across his shoulders as the wind settled. The vamps before him had been *GQ* in their dress. He was more motorcycle mag in his black T-shirt and jeans. He crouched beside me, his expression curious. "Stake in the ass?" he asked, his voice thick with a French accent. Although I didn't answer, but rather growled and tried to claw him, he nodded. "I hate it when that happens."

He yanked it out before I could move. I fought not to roar, beating my fists against the ground.

The vamp examined the stake closely. Like all of Shayna's makeshift weapons, it failed to keep its form, returning to a small twisted twig in his hand. He sniffed the blood. "Interesting," he said, before tossing it over his shoulder. "Now tell me, *mon ami*. Where is Giovanna?"

I scrambled to my feet, grabbing my butt as if it could fall off, and doing my damnedest to ignore the puncture wounds burning their way across my shoulders. My sisters and Danny hurried to step in front of me. Shayna tossed me her gray sweater while the vamp continued to eye us with interest.

I released my cheek enough to yank on her sweater. Danny and my sisters had seen me naked before. That didn't mean I was comfortable being unclothed and vulnerable. Especially with another predator so close.

The vamp frowned slightly. "You will not tell me?" He motioned to the closest mound of ash. "Why do you protect her?"

"Who?" Shayna asked.

"You do not know of whom I speak?"

"No." Shayna glanced around. "None of us know a Giovanna."

The vamp angled his chin again, more curious then threatening, and sniffed the air.

"What the hell is he doing?" Taran muttered to Danny.

"Smelling the air. Preternaturals can scent lies."

The vamp smiled. "That is true. Seeing your lack of knowledge, perhaps I ask the wrong beings, no?"

He stalked a few feet away into the section of knee-deep dry grass. It was strange that he gave us his back. He obviously didn't fear us, either because he was too stupid or he was too lethal. Knowing our luck, he wasn't the dumb prick I wanted him to be.

He spread the blades of tall grass aside until he found what he was looking for. He then stood, holding a vamp's severed head by the tuft of his curly hair. I recognized him as the one Shayna had chased and evidently decapitated. We jumped when the head's eyes whipped open and he snapped his fangs at the vamp.

Again, this wouldn't have happened to Buffy.

The biker-clad vamp shook his head as if reprimanding a naughty child. "Ah, Dunbar, you try my patience. Now tell me, where is your lovely Giovanna?"

"Eat my mother's shit, Quennel. I shall not betray my mistress!"

Quennel nodded. "Perhaps you are correct." He tossed the head. It rolled in our direction like a ball with chunky skin and stopped at our feet, hissing at us.

My sisters screamed and so did Danny. I gaped at it, not wanting to believe what I saw. The thing was spitting mad, snarling and chomping at the air. Shayna went into complete freak-out mode. She grabbed a small branch and bashed the head like a kid hell-bent on cracking open a piñata.

"Harder!" Taran shrieked. *"Harder.* Oh, *Gawd,* it's eating the stick!"

The head clenched the branch between its fangs. Shayna shook the branch, making the head bop and bounce until the tip snapped off and the head spun toward Emme. She jumped behind me, screaming while pieces of wood oozed from the vamp's split neck.

Quennel appeared beside me, startling us yet again. "What strange creatures you are indeed, little ones. But I fear your tactics won't suffice. Allow me."

He jogged down the field and cut left. The head hollered, "No, no, *no!*" as the remainder of his body rose from another patch of overgrown field and bolted toward the neighborhood.

Quennel raced after it with little effort, grabbed it by the shoulders, and punched through his sternum.

The body exploded into a cloud of ash, just like the abandoned head on the ground. Our stares traveled from it back to Quennel, who leisurely returned to our side.

"A vamp over three hundred years old requires both decapitation and destruction of the heart," he said. "Lesson learned, no?"

We nodded in unison, all of us appearing at a loss for words. I moved forward, still suspicious of our latest visitor. "If you're not with these vamps, what are you doing here?"

"I tracked Giovanna's family, when they tracked him." He sniffed in Danny's direction. "You are the son of Joseph Matagrano?"

"Uh, yeah. He's my dad."

"Did Giovanna take him as her keep?"

"Keep?" Danny asked.

Quennel smiled, showing a little fang. "Someone a master vampire controls—a vampire he creates, or a human he regularly feeds from. Were they lovers?"

Danny's skin blanched. "I don't know. My father is a well-known attorney. I think he might have represented Giovanna for something a while back; but he doesn't date, even though my mother died over a decade ago."

"He may not have wanted Giovanna, *mon ami*. But vampires are hard to resist."

"I can see that," Taran mumbled. "Well, I'm not blind, Celia," she snapped upon catching my glare. "Did you see what they looked like?"

"Before or after they tried to eat us?" I hissed.

Quennel chuckled. "Nature has been kind to us. Our scent, our looks, it's our way of attracting food so it comes to us willingly. Otherwise we are not permitted to take."

"I wasn't willing just now," I added with a growl. "One of these vamps tried to bite me, and he didn't care whether I'd deny him."

"Yes, it has been rumored that Giovanna ignores our laws and takes as she pleases." Quennel's irises darkened. "But to allow her family to do the same? This is very bad for her."

Shayna grimaced at the mound of ash that used to be a snarling head. "How bad?" She pointed to the pile. "This bad?"

"Mm. There has been talk that she's unhealthy in the head, shall we say?" He pursed his full lips. "The courts won't bother hearing her pleas now. And I'm under no obligation to show her mercy."

Danny's face brightened. "So, you're here to help me—to save my dad? Thank *God*. He's really weak. I think she's been draining him of his blood and—"

Quennel raised his hand, silencing him. "My presence is not on your behalf. It's on behalf of my master, Angelo Cusamano. He *turned* me decades ago. Like him, I am a master. Should I kill Giovanna as he asks, I'll inherit her keep, her power, and her domain."

I gave him a hard stare. "So you're only out for yourself?"

He smiled. "Humans are food to me. Not pets, or anything to distress over. As a vampire, I am not allowed to kill you—only to take the small amounts of blood I need to nourish myself. But that does not oblige me to save you. Only *weres* carry that burden."

"So, you won't help me." Danny's voice cracked with frustration and hurt. If Giovanna had claimed his father as Quennel believed, God only knew what she was subjecting him to.

Quennel watched him. "No, but I tell you this, young Matagrano. Should my killing Giovanna result in your father's freedom, it would benefit us both, no?" He reached into his back pocket and handed him a business card. "If you find her, tell me. I'll do the same for you and perhaps we'll both obtain what we want." He waited while Danny called his phone so he'd have his number, then turned and walked away. He'd only taken a few steps before he paused and glanced over his shoulder. "I urge you to find your father quickly. If Giovanna is fixated on him, she'll attempt to *turn* him. If he's as weak as you claim, he won't survive the bite

Chapter Four

My hands split the kitchen table in half. Taran grunted, "Damn it, Celia, try and keep still, Emme's almost done." She held one arm, Shayna the other. Neither could keep me still despite using the full weight of their petite bodies.

It didn't feel like Emme was almost done. Her torturous attempts at healing had me jolting and growling. My butt and face burned as if branded, and my shoulders begged me to saw them off. It was all I could do not to bolt. Tears spilled down my face as the bones of my face realigned with a sickening crunch and the holes in my shoulders filled in.

After what felt like an hour of torment, the relentless throbbing slowly subsided. "Oops," Emme said.

My spine stiffened. "Oops? What do you mean by 'oops'?"

Shayna shoved her face in mine. "Well, your butt sort of looks like you were attacked by a lion." She looked back. "With braces." Another glance. "And he seriously kicked your ass."

"Fabulous." But it wasn't like anyone but me would miss the old cheek.

I tried to remember how to breathe as I stumbled into our bedroom and slipped on a new shirt and a pair of jeans. "You can come back in, Danny," I called. When I returned to the kitchen, I slumped into the closest chair, grateful I could at least sit.

Emme wrung her hands. "Um. Sorry, Celia. I wish I was better at this sort of thing."

I waved off her apology. Emme was sweet, and meant well. That's why she'd done so well as a hospice nurse, and why she'd continue in that field when we moved. If we moved. And if we didn't die. Damn, what a night.

She made her way to Danny's side and clasped his shoulder. "Sorry you had to wait, but don't worry. You won't take as long as poor Celia."

Danny rubbed his bruised throat, his hesitation spreading across his face. "Uh, that's okay, Emme. I'm good."

"Are you sure?"

"Positive." He sighed as he took in our somber expressions. "Listen. I know I shouldn't have dragged you into this mess—"

"No kidding, Danny!" Taran pulled at her destroyed shirt and then shook out bark and blades of grass from her hair, irritated. Her fire had caused patches of grass to burn. Since she was immune to her flame, she had rolled herself across the grass to extinguish it. Let's just say she wasn't in the cheeriest mood. "This whole thing is a shit storm with no end in sight."

"God, I know, and I'm so sorry."

"You're sorry? Really? Is that all you have to say?" She crossed her arms. "Because of the vamps' super sniffing powers, they can track us from the field, right back here. Just like they freaking tracked you from Warren!"

"Taran, stop it."

She whipped around. "Stop what, Celia? Speaking the goddamn truth? We are totally screwed here."

"Not as bad as Danny and his father are," I ground out. "We're leaving. They're not. And they have no way to protect themselves."

Bolts of blue and white lightning fired above her head. "Neither do we." She pointed to the dwindling sparks. "The element of surprise is gone now. Do you honestly think we'll all survive if they show up again?"

I didn't answer her. Mostly because I knew she was right.

Except for the rattle of our old radiators kicking in and our soft breaths, there was no other sound for a long while. Danny rapped his knuckles against the table, his hand trembling. "I'm sorry. I never meant for any of you to be harmed. I thought with your powers, you'd be more formidable and no way could they hurt you." He focused on me, his eyes glistening. "You always seemed so strong, Celia. I just never realized how much stronger these vamps would be."

Danny's heart was breaking. I could see it by the way his face shadowed with misery. My own heart ached to see him this way. "I only seemed stronger compared to a human, Danny. We held our own tonight but mostly we were lucky." I wiped the leftover blood from my nose. "I just don't know if we're enough to help you and your dad."

Shayna busied herself making chai tea and poured it into the old yellow ceramic mugs that had been a part of the house for as long as I could remember. She paused as she tipped the teapot over Danny's mug. "Ceel's right. We're not strong enough to help anyone, not like this. But I think there's a way we can be." She set the teapot down on the table. "What say we break this bind thingy he's talking about?"

She said it like most frat boys ask, "Who wants a beer?"

We all stared at her.

Shayna held her hands out. "Hear me out. As you know, I can learn to wield any weapon just by watching it once—in a movie or on TV. And I can manipulate anything metal or wood. But my aim has been sucky forever, no matter how hard I try to improve it. What you don't know is how heavy my arms feel the minute I start swinging or how sometimes I feel this strange pull on my wrists."

"So?" Taran asked, her voice more annoyed than usual.

"*So,* I used to accept it as a limitation to my power, but after what Danny said, I don't think it is. Now, take Taran for instance." She ignored Taran's glare. "Her fire and lightning pizzazz stay with her. Shouldn't she able to fire that puppy up or out? You know, like a bullet or something? Same thing with Celia and Emme. Something is holding us all back, dudes. I say we do something about it." She smiled sadly at Danny. "We can't just walk away, you know?"

I dumped my tea out into the old porcelain sink and leaned over it, gripping the edge tight while I thought matters through. Shayna was right. The vamps who held Danny's father were ruthless. They didn't care that Danny and his father were human and incapable of fighting back. If anything, the Matagranos had been targeted because of their weakness. We had to do something. "Tell us what we need to do to get your father back."

"You'll help me?"

I nodded.

"Thank you, Celia. Thank you so much." Danny removed his glasses to wipe his grateful tears. "He's all that I have left."

I released the sink. "I don't want to be stupid about things. But I also know we don't have a lot of time."

Danny rubbed his hands nervously. "I know. Tell me everything you know about the curse. Maybe it could help me understand the bind more."

My sisters turned to me. I tightened my jaw. This so wasn't going to be a good time. I left the kitchen and walked into the family room, itching with the need to move, but knowing I couldn't go far. Everyone followed. I flopped onto the loveseat and thought about where to begin. The subject of our parents' deaths always put me on edge. As the oldest, I remembered the most—my mother's laugh, my father's grin when he played with us, and how much they adored us. I also remembered their lifeless bodies following their murders. They never stood a chance against those gangbangers who broke into our home. Just like Danny and his father didn't stand a chance now without us.

"Celia?" Emme prodded gently.

I reeled in my emotions and tried to soften my hardening features. "Our mother described the rest of her Latino family as tight-knit. But she believed her family resented her lighter tones and she never felt accepted." I swallowed hard. "When she married our father, her family disowned her and accused her of abandoning her race. The curse appears to be their way of punishing her."

I took a breath to squelch my growing anger and tame the big kitty within me who was suddenly alert. "There was a day when one of our aunts showed up at our door. She was so furious with Mom." I looked at Emme. "I must have been almost four, because I remember Mom being pregnant with you. She was far along, big belly, and obviously vulnerable, but this woman didn't seem to care. She screamed until Mom slammed the door in her face."

Shayna squirmed a little, and lowered her head. "Do you remember anything she said?"

In my anger at my mother's treatment, my tone was harder than I intended. "She said Mom was wrong to have us. That we should've never been born."

Taran glanced up then. "Nice. Real fuckin' nice. What did the crazy bitch look like?"

I thought about it. Crap, I was so little. "Plump and about fortyish, I guess. But her eyes were what's seared into my brain. They were black—so black they didn't seem to have irises."

"Could she have been the one to curse us?"

Taran waited for me to answer her. I tapped my foot, trying to decide. But when it came down to it, I didn't know for certain. "It's hard to say. The thing that stays with me the most about the incident was her eyes.

They didn't seem quite right. It wasn't just the color, the woman seemed . . . odd."

"Crazy-eyed?" Taran offered.

"More like murderous."

Everyone gasped. My tigress eyes were flaring, and I blinked them back, returning them to their normal shape and color.

Danny sighed heavily, the sound cutting through the tension. "I know this is hard, and I'm not trying to make it harder, but can you tell me about the actual curse? Did your mother ever mention the words used?"

I stiffened a little. "She did."

Emme glanced around. "I don't recall that."

"Maybe you just don't remember because you were so young." My fingertips itched. It wouldn't be long before my claws would protrude. "The words aren't pretty, and the tone's malicious. If you don't want to hear them, Danny and I can go into another room."

Emme appeared torn. Not Taran. "Screw it, Celia. Just tell us. We can't hide from this shit."

I didn't immediately speak, struggling to recall the exact words. "The first part was directed at Mom and Dad, and was something like 'You will not know the years ahead of you and will die with the man who poisoned your family. You will bleed and know the pain only death can bring. You will feel your blood as it leaves you. You will ache with every last pulse. I swear on my life you will know only agony.'"

I waited, letting them take it all in.

"Ceel! That was totally . . . *horrid*." Shayna's face paled. "Was there, like, *more*?"

"The rest was all us. Are you sure you want to hear it?" At their collective nods, I cleared my throat and finished. "'Your children will devour blades and weep like weak and sickly runts. Predators will hunt them to pierce their flesh with fang and claw. They will burn with fire and hide from shame, for nowhere will they find strength, or love, or kindness.'"

Cue the eerie and dumbstruck silence.

"Aw, hell," Taran said after a few moments. "As far as curses go, that was pretty damn evil."

"You think?" I stood, shaking out my hands and claws.

Danny's face was buried in his hands. I guessed he was mulling over the curse. He remained quiet, then, without warning, his head popped up and he rushed to me. Excitement stirred behind the thick lenses of his glasses. "It backfired!" he said.

I raised my eyebrows and motioned around the room. "Uh, I don't think so. Our parents are dead, Danny. And kindness and love have eluded us—just like the curse intended. We've never had friends and have been mercilessly berated. Remember I told you our classmates nicknamed us the "weird girls" — and it wasn't just because our last name is Wird."

Danny pointed at me. "But the rest didn't come true."

Taran huffed. "Were you not listening?" She began to count off with her fingers. "Weak and sickly runts—Emme was born premature and spent the first six weeks of her life in the NICU."

"Learning to heal," Danny said like it was obvious.

This gave Taran pause, but then she added another finger. "Your children will devour blades—"

Danny interrupted. "What happens when you devour something?"

Taran glared at him.

"Come on, tell me what happens."

"It's broken down and absorbed into my body's system . . ."

Her voice trailed as Shayna unfolded her legs and rose slowly. "Like how I absorb the metal I'm wearing and transfer it."

"I was given the fire." Taran's voice was barely audible.

Everyone suddenly watched me. I stared at my claws. "And I'm the predator who hunts, piercing flesh with fang and claw."

Danny held out his hands. "There's a theory that the world maintains magic at a delicate balance—especially when it comes to dark power and causing harm. For the most part, it's believed the earth's magic is pure. I think it must have intercepted the spell cast against you."

"How?" Shayna asked, her expression split between excitement and confusion.

"No idea," Danny said. "But let me finish. Your parents were cursed with death, and I'm sorry that came true. *Jesus*. I'm really sorry. But in analyzing the severity of your aunt's words, I believe the part of the curse directed at the rest of you also meant to kill. For some inexplicable reason, though, this aunt wanted you to suffer longer. Maybe she intended for you to have an illness—be eaten by a pack of rabid dogs, commit suicide by swallowing razor blades—I don't know. But whatever it was didn't work. It gave you strength and power."

Numbness claimed me; something was wrong. "How come I didn't realize the curse had backfired before? It seems so obvious now that we're talking about it."

Danny placed his hands on my shoulders. "I believe it's part of the bind. Think about it. You have these abilities that you've never discussed. Maybe you weren't meant to discuss them. Maybe you weren't meant to understand any of it." He sighed. "If you can't recognize what's holding you back, you can't exactly move forward."

Shayna jumped out of her seat. "Hold up. You're saying we were also whammied with something that kept us quiet and in the dark?"

"I can't think of another explanation. Can you?" We all shook our heads. Danny's stare turned intense. I could almost picture the synapses of his brilliant mind firing. "This was a death spell—a powerful one because it extended to six people. When it backfired, she must have sensed it and bound you."

Taran stared at Danny as if she'd been slapped. "Damn, but . . . now what?"

Danny addressed Taran. "No matter how strong this witch—your aunt, I mean—is or was, she can't maintain the bind without building an altar for it."

"Altar?" Emme asked.

"Something that keeps the bind going whether she's alive or dead. Destroy the altar, and you cut loose the bind."

"Okay . . ." I said. This wasn't a lot to take in or anything. "But how do we find it?"

Danny grinned. "Leave that to me"

Chapter Five

My sisters and I didn't grow up attending family gatherings, holiday dinners, or whatever it is people who have normal families do. So, we hadn't expected a warm welcome from any relative we came across. However, we never anticipated, well, *this:*

"*Diablas!*"

Devils. The old woman clutching a rosary had called us devils. It was bad enough she pelted Taran in the head with a cluster of garlic.

The other six apartment doors we'd knocked on in the roach-infested building had been slammed in our faces. And don't get me started on the one woman who fell to her knees, begging God to banish our apparently unholy asses from her threshold.

My heart raced as we hurried out of the dilapidated building and to our car. We were running out of time to help Danny's father.

I speed-dialed Danny and put him on speaker phone the second he answered.

"How's it going, Celia?" he asked, his voice rushed.

"Shitty," Taran muttered. "I don't think that spell of yours worked."

We'd left him at our house staring at a piece of paper floating in a clear glass bowl. I heard him turn a page from the book he referenced. "Hmmm. According to Old Norse legend, this locating spell should work for anyone—even if he or she is not a being of magic."

Shayna picked a clove of garlic from Taran's hair. "It's not that we're not in the right place, little guy," she said. "People around here seem to sense who we are. It's just that we're not finding any leads, or anyone willing to help us." Her head jerked back to the building, her nervous energy building enough that I could scent it.

"The triangle in the water isn't moving," Danny insisted. "If it moved right or left, I could tell you where to go, just as I did to get you to Plainfield in the first place. You have to be in the right place."

I remained on alert. I'd never expected to return to the same city where my parents had been killed, and where I'd avenged them. But there I was, thanks to Danny's mystical navigation system. He'd pricked our fingers and added our blood into the clear bowl with *North, South, East,* and *West* printed at its base with marker.

Nothing happened until he placed our only photo of our parents in front of a lighted candle and chanted a few words I couldn't make out. The small triangle of paper spun and shot to the "east" side of the bowl and off we went, scared and pressed for time but determined to see matters through. Taran had driven, while Danny instructed us via cell phone. I almost hurled when we veered off Route 22 and took the Plainfield exit.

Emme said, "Is it possible the compass needle—or whatever you called it—didn't stop because the spell ran out of power?"

"Ouch!" Danny yelled.

"Are you okay?" I asked him.

"Uh, yeah. I tried to move the paper—the compass needle, I mean—back to the edge to test Emme's theory. I don't think the spell liked being doubted. The paper . . . *stung* me and returned to the center, where it's been floating."

"The little piece of paper bit you?" Taran didn't wait for Danny to answer. "Shit, then what's this goddamn bind thing going to do to us if we ever find the altar?"

"Hi, Celia."

I don't know who jumped higher, me or Emme. No one snuck up on me. Ever. And yet there stood a young woman with two waist-length pigtails and large-framed red glasses with lenses thicker than Danny's. Crap, she was thin. Knobby knees poked out beneath a long pink T-shirt big enough to serve as a dress; its V neck accentuated her bony chest and barely-there bosom.

She removed her glasses and wiped her eyes. I'd never seen eyes as light as hers. The green tinge in them was barely noticeable. If anything, they appeared colorless, like a blank canvas waiting to be filled.

She returned her glasses to her face. "I'm sorry. Did I scare you, Celia?"

My sisters gathered beside me. "How do you know my name?"

She smiled gently, though it appeared more of a polite gesture than anything genuine. She seemed tired. More tired than a twenty-something girl should look. Deep blue veins gathered around the creases of her sunken eyes. She lowered her voice. "Everyone in the family knows who you are. Even though we're not supposed to speak of you, or Taran, or Shayna, or Emme." Her attention bounced to my sisters with each of their names until she returned it fully to me. "I'm your cousin, Nieve."

"Nee-yeh-vay?" Emme asked slowly. "As in 'snow'?"

Nieve nodded, but stopped smiling. "I'm surprised you'd return here. Especially after all that's been done to keep you away."

"You know about us—about our curse." Taran's voice was as hard as marble and just as cold. "How is that possible when we don't know a damn thing about you?"

Sadness dulled Nieve's unusually fair skin. "I told you. We all know who you are. You're the ones who weren't meant to be."

Taran huffed and crossed her arms. "So we've heard. Are you going to tell us more, or are you having fun pretending to be all mysterious?"

Shayna nudged Taran, fearing her attitude would intimidate Nieve. She recognized that Nieve was our only lead and how much we needed her then.

Nieve kept her head lowered, appearing to choose her words carefully. "My grandmother told me Tía Griselda never liked your mother. Tía was the one who riled the others against your mother and accused her of bringing the darkness."

My fists clenched and so did my jaw. I had to work not to growl. "If that's the case, Griselda lied. Our mother was kind and good. There was nothing dark about her."

A tear slid from Nieve's eyes, but my instincts told me her reaction didn't stem from fear of me. "Truth doesn't always matter, Celia. Especially if there are enough willing to believe the lies."

"And especially against one who's already ostracized," I added, trying to soften my tone.

Another tear streaked Nieve's cheek. "You're right. Tía Griselda carried evil in her heart, and her spirit, but she made sure her poison wasn't so obvious that it warned others away. She would smile and say all the right things, attracting with her looks and her sweet words, all the while demonstrating power no one could match or hide from. Dark power only dared spoken of in whispers."

Taran kicked at a pebble on the sidewalk. It rolled beneath our sedan. "This Tía Griselda, I take it she's the batshit crazy bitch who cursed us?"

Nieve glanced around as if waiting for someone to appear. "None of our relatives possessed magical abilities. She became the first when she married into our family. She was a well-known witch—born and raised of magic. Many found her fascinating and the majority who knew her sought to win her favor. But anyone who tasted even a speck of her power rightfully feared her. No one messed with her or her children. Horrible things happened to those who attempted to stand against them."

Shayna stilled. "There's more than one—besides Griselda?"

Nieve pressed her finger to her lips. "Shhhh. It's best not to speak of them too much. Tía Gris is dead. But her legacy continues." She shuddered. "Her children are not kind souls. Like Tia, they invoke respect through fear. Believe me when I say you don't want to get on their bad side."

Nieve inched away from me as I watched her closely. "Why are you telling us this?" I asked. "If you're this afraid, why get involved?"

She played with the ends of her long braids. "There are a few in our family who believe your mother was harshly condemned. These same recognize Tía Gris's power as the darkness she accused your mother of harboring. I think Tía saw something in your mother. Something she felt would threaten her and her lineage. Maybe it was the four of you. I can't be certain. But whatever it was, she meant to stop it. She liked her power, and wanted to keep it. But in lashing out against your mother, she created you. Beings who weren't meant to be."

"Because we threatened her power," I finished for her.

"Maybe," Nieve said. "Maybe not. But her actions seem to say as much."

Emme stepped forward and attempted to take Nieve's hand, but Nieve jerked from her reach.

"I'm sorry, Nieve," Emme said. "I didn't mean to frighten you. But you seem so . . . weak."

Nieve rubbed her arms as if cold, but didn't comment.

Taran clasped Emme's arm and pulled her back, her stare narrowing with growing suspicion. "You didn't answer Celia's question. You're obviously scared shitless. So why are you involved? Why are you feeding us all this information? And don't tell me it's just because I asked."

Nieve pressed her lips tight as she appeared to gather her courage. Her voice cracked when she spoke, revealing the depths of both her sadness and fear. "Because curses are meant to be broken. It's time you broke yours and embraced the full scope of your power."

"Son of a bitch, I don't like this," Taran said as she and I walked side by side, behind Nieve and in front of Shayna and Emme.

"I don't like this either, Taran. But she knows more than we do." I swore. "If Quennel and Danny are right, his father doesn't have much longer."

Shayna hurried to catch up. "Do you think his dad's already dead?"

"I don't know. If he's not, he soon will be." The thought made me walk faster.

"What if it's a trap?" Emme whispered.

That question had crossed my mind several times. But each time I considered whether it was best for us to hightail it out of there, I reached the same conclusion. "Danny's in a lot of trouble—and so are we if we don't break this bind trapping us. We have no other leads right now and therefore no choices. But just in case, stay sharp."

"This whole thing is horseshit," Taran grumbled. She stared ahead at the rows of once majestic Victorians that lined either side of the street, two blocks from the apartment complex on Madison Avenue where we first began our search. Now the homes waited impatiently for a fresh coat of paint, a new roof, and tenants who would care enough to tidy their garbage-strewn yards.

Two men in gang colors made an exchange—money for a clear package filled with white powder—while the little girl in the yard with them skipped rope. The men watched my sisters and me, knowing we weren't from around there. They ignored Nieve, who strolled in her bare feet and oversized shirt as if she'd walked along this street a thousand times. Shards of glass littered the sidewalk, but she simply skipped around the slivers.

Nieve didn't act like a mature, young woman, nor did she take much pride in her appearance. Her braids, although neat, were tied with rubber bands, and her T-shirt was old and stained. Though she was intelligent and articulate, something about her suggested she knew little about life. Strange considering the harsh and dangerous area she lived in.

"Hey, blondie," one of the men called to Emme. "Do you want some of this, boo?"

"No, she doesn't," I said.

The initial hard stares the men shot my way contorted into looks of surprise and instant fear. My tigress had risen to the surface the moment Nieve had arrived. And while my inner beast hadn't perceived her as a threat, she did the men. With a growl that thumped against my throat, she urged me in their direction.

The moisture in my mouth building from the thought of tasting their blood made me ill. And still she moved us forward when one of the men lifted his shirt to show me the gun shoved into his waistband. Tough guy. Ballsy even. Or so he thought, until my tigress poked out enough to show a hint of her eyes and a glimmer of fang.

My new pals found somewhere else to be. The idiot with the piece bolted down the street while the addict grabbed the little girl and raced them both into the house. They would probably dismiss or minimize what they saw later. But for now, they had believed the threat, just as my beast had intended.

Nieve didn't turn around when she spoke. "Your fearlessness will take you far, Celia. Especially for what awaits you." She cut a sharp left, up a small incline, and into a yard where patches of yellow grass intermixed with the clusters of dandelions. Steps led up to a ramshackle house competing for the title of most likely to hide dead bodies and serial killers. Four to five smaller apartments made up the Victorian. Tarnished metal bars covered every window while tarp and pieces of nailed-down plywood covered part of the roof. A family of pigeons gathered near the crumbling chimney, cooing to the setting sun. It saddened me to see a once lovely piece of architecture reduced to scraps, but what saddened me more was knowing people actually lived there.

"This is it," Nieve called over her shoulder.

Shayna wrenched her head up as we advanced. "Holy creepy mansion, Batman."

Yup. I only wished Batman had come along for the ass-kicking.

But Nieve didn't hurry up the wooden steps like we expected. Instead she remained on the grass, walking alongside the wraparound porch and into the side yard. We trailed quickly behind her until she stopped at the rusty gate of an old chain-link fence.

Nieve stared ahead at what appeared to be a converted garage. Strips of peeling white paint barely clung to the graying wood and grime coated the narrow windows. The building was smaller, and in many ways in better condition, than the main house. But something about it colored my mind with images of bleeding walls.

Nieve motioned with a small jerk of her chin, keeping her trembling voice soft. "Tía Gris was known to worship in there. It houses remnants of the spells she cast—remnants of her power. The altar you seek may be in there, since it would require her energy to maintain, especially now that she's dead."

"Is she for sure dead?" Shayna asked. "I mean, if she was as strong as you say, I find it hard to believe she's not still kickin' around."

"Oh, I'm sure she would still be with us if it hadn't been for the incident."

"Incident?" Emme asked almost inaudibly.

Nieve nodded. "She angered a werewolf and he tore out her throat."

"Oh," the rest of us answered in unison, our voices unusually shrill.

I rubbed my hands together, trying to work through my rush of adrenaline. "Okay . . . okay. Say the altar isn't in there. Then what?"

Nieve shuddered. "If it's not there, it'll be in her old house." She backed away from the gate, wrapping her arms tightly around herself. "I'm sorry, *primas*. I won't go there."

"Then let's just hope the altar's inside. Come on." Taran reached for the gate's latch. The minute her hand connected, her blue eyes bleached to white. Pure white. No irises. No borders. Nothing but space.

Shayna's and Emme's mouths popped open. I shook Taran's shoulder, hoping the color would adjust. Nope. "Well, it looks like we're in the right place."

Taran threw the gate open and shook out her hand. "No shit, Celia." She blew out a very deep breath. "Friggin' hocus pocus. Let's do this and get back to Danny."

No one moved. Except Nieve, who raced to the front of the house. "I'll wait here, *primas,*" she shouted. "Good luck."

"Th-that's kind of sweet that she refers to us as 'cousins,'" Emme said in lieu of charging into action.

Shayna's head jerked from the old garage back to where Nieve had disappeared. "I just hope she won't refer to us as dead *primas* before this is all done. Man, that building looks totally Freddy Krueger."

As if on cue, a flock of bats—that's right, *bats*—soared from a large hole in the crumbling garage's belfry. We dove onto the ground as they flew over our heads in a mess of snapping fangs and flapping wings, screeching with angst. My flesh crawled along my bones. There was spooky, and there was this. Good Lord, I wanted to race to the nearest church and douse myself with holy water.

The minute their disturbing squeaks died down, Taran scrambled to her feet. "Screw *this*!"

I latched onto her elbow when she attempted to flee. "Taran. We've made it this far. If this binding spell does exist, we have to break it. For us and for Danny."

Her crumpling face told me how very frightened my usually tough sister was. I didn't want to force any of them, but this curse affected us all.

"Please, Taran," Emme pleaded. "Danny needs us."

Taran nodded at Emme and I squeezed her arm reassuringly. No matter what, they would make it out of this mess. Even if it meant without me.

Shayna ignored all of us and dug around the shrubs. Something had caught her attention. I expected her to withdraw a stick she could convert into a sword with her power. Instead she pulled out an old wooden Louisville Slugger and transformed it into a giant battle-ax.

"What?" she asked when we all gaped at her and her weapon of mass destruction. "Did you see those little flying critters? Evil's afoot, dudettes. I'm not walking in there without my little friend here."

"Uh, okay." I cleared my throat. "Emme, call Danny and put him on speaker. Then tuck your phone into your back pocket with the speaker out so we can all hopefully hear him."

She nodded and did as I asked.

Danny answered immediately. "How's it going? You girls okay?"

"We're here," Shayna said, mimicking the little kid from *Poltergeist*. She yelped when Taran smacked her arm.

I stepped through the gate, wondering if anyone would follow. By some miracle, each of my sisters did, with Shayna skipping ahead with her battle-ax. Sometimes, I really wondered about her.

"We'll leave you on speaker in case we need you," I said.

"All right, but please be careful. This altar has to be destroyed by your hands in order to free you from the bind."

"How will we know if it's the right one?" Emme asked hesitantly. "What if it's someone else's altar?"

I groaned. "Emme has a point. I don't want to accidently free hell's minions. We're in enough trouble."

"I think you girls will know for sure. Everything I've read says altars designed to bind are identifiable to those held. It goes back to the rule of maintaining balance. If it's cast on someone, that person has to at least be given the opportunity to recognize it."

"Well, let's hope you're right." I reached the garage and stood on my tippy-toes, trying in vain to peer through the grimy and darkened glass. "I can't see anything. It looks like there're plastic garbage bags taped to the window. Let's go around. There has to be a side door."

Shayna skipped ahead, finding a door around the corner. Deadbolts lined almost the entire rim of the wooden door. "Can you break it, Ceel?" She lifted her battle-ax. "If not, I can use Junior here."

Taran pointed at her. "What I think you should do is calm the hell down. You're a little too excited here, princess."

Shayna grinned. "I just know we're close. We're going to get control over our magic and save Danny's dad. I'm sure of it!"

Taran huffed. "I just don't want to be eaten. Son of bitch, is that too much to ask for?"

Emme inched closer to Shayna and her little friend, peering over her shoulder. "I hope not," she mumbled.

I held up my hand to silence them. My gaze cut side to side and my ears took everything in, focusing on our immediate surroundings. For a crowded neighborhood within a large city, all seemed a little too quiet. "I think I should break it down in case there's something waiting for us inside." I took in the number of locks I needed to bust through. "But it's going to make a lot of noise."

Taran rolled her eyes. "You're worried about someone reporting a breaking and entering out here? Trust me, these peeps learned to keep their mouths shut a long time ago."

"Good point." My sisters gave me plenty of space as I whipped my foot back. Fear must have fueled my strength; I kicked the door from its frame with just a few strikes.

Thick musty air carried dust and the bitter stench of menace into my nose, making me sneeze. My eyes searched through the darkness. This wasn't just a place of worship, it was a crypt laced with suffering and pieces of the dead.

Black candles in clear glass gathered in rows formed a circle at the center of the room, while skulls in varying sizes lined the shelves encasing the perimeter. It was obvious that no one had entered this place in years, and yet the flames flickering from the candles had barely chewed through the wicks. Griselda's residual magic must have been feeding the candles' energy.

"H-how is it in there?"

I think Emme had expected dead squirrels hanging from nooses. Hell, so had I. "Creepy, definitely creepy. But aside from the skulls lining the shelves and some candles, it's not so bad."

Or it wasn't until I stepped inside and so did my sisters. The air popped in sections like a cluster of balloons, releasing the rancid aroma of death. Torturous, bloodcurdling death. We gagged, trying to beat down the sudden surge of nausea.

Something moist and sticky landed at the center of the circle. I fixed my gaze straight ahead. Nothing that smelled this bad was worth seeing. My tigress insisted otherwise and forced my head up.

My body staggered backward and my knees threatened to buckle. "Oh . . . *God.*"

My sisters glanced up, muffling their screams. Terror kept me quiet and slammed my mouth shut.

A woman lay sprawled against the ceiling, anchored in place by nine-inch nails. Decomposing flesh slid along the metal shafts, splattering the concrete below while we stood frozen by the sheer brutality. Railroad spikes had been driven through her breasts, eyes, and belly button, and words were carved into her skin. NO SEE etched into her forehead. NO BREED lanced across her belly. NO COMFORT sliced above her breasts.

She'd suffered long and hard. And despite the spikes blinding her and indenting her skull, she bore an uncanny resemblance.

To me.

Chapter Six

My breath came out in a shudder and my eyes burned. *It's not you,* I told myself. *It's not you.* I repeated the phrase over and over. Too bad I didn't believe me.

"Hello? Hello? Are you girls okay?" Danny's shaky voice echoed through the dimness.

"No. No! We're not fucking okay." Taran's speech mixed with gags. "There is a goddamn woman nailed to the goddamn ceiling and she fucking looks like Celia!"

"Oh, God. It must be the altar."

"You're just a friggin' genius, aren't you, asshole!"

Another lump of skin fell. Loud enough to be a foot.

Taran spit on the concrete. "Son of a bastard's ass . . . I'm going to hurl."

"Okay . . . okay . . . okay . . . t-tell me what's happening."

I beat back the burn of my roiling stomach. "The woman is falling apart in . . . in . . . *chunks*."

Danny coughed as if unable to stand the thought. "That's just . . . *wrong*." He coughed a few more times and sounded as if he were shuddering. "But believe it or not, it's a good sign."

A larger portion fell. Shayna clutched her battle-ax against her like a child would a teddy bear. "Oh . . . I don't think so, little guy."

"You may not believe me, but the woman is not real," Danny said soothingly. "She's a culmination of the suffering your aunt caused."

"Then why does she look like me?" I couldn't stop my hands from trembling.

"I think because you're the strongest, and the leader of your family. If there was a war, and the first to suffer was the general, the soldiers would panic. The image of you there is meant to cause fear and dread."

Even through the darkness, I could see Emme's soft green eyes water. "Well, it worked," I told him.

Danny swallowed hard, tears of regret heavy in his voice. "I'm so sorry I did this to you, Celia, to *all* of you. Believe me when I say my research of the curse was intended only to help you—not to cause you distress or pain." He sighed. "If you don't want to do this, *don't*. Get out now. I'll figure something else out to help my dad."

I watched the candles burn. Griselda was dead, and still she mocked us with her spell-work, keeping us firmly within her magical grasp. I took in my sisters with narrowing eyes. "If we don't do this, Gris still has us and we'll never be free."

Shayna adjusted her hold on her battle-ax. "Ceel's right. This whole thing started out as a totally evil spite against us. But it doesn't have to stay that way. We can use it to our advantage and totally kick her in the tush."

We waited for Emme and Taran to speak. As much as Shayna and I thought the destruction was necessary, we couldn't charge forward without them. This was a family problem. And every member needed to agree.

Emme finally stepped forward. "Griselda's curse killed Mom and Dad. Who's to say this bind won't eventually strangle us if we don't sever it?" She stroked my hand with hers. "She meant for us to die, didn't she?"

"She did," I answered.

She pursed her soft pink lips. "Well, I want to live. Don't you?"

Emme never spoke much. But when she did, she was typically profound. Taran quirked a perfect brow her way. "Tell us what we need to do, Danny," she said. "Just 'cause we lost our family doesn't mean you should lose yours, too."

Danny sighed. "Are you sure?"

The candles flickered as if taunting us. I cracked my knuckles. "Yeah. We're sure."

"Okay." He riffled through his notes. "You said there are candles, right?"

"Yes," I answered.

"Black or red?"

"Black."

He let out a breath. "Destroy all the candles, and you break the bind."

I lifted the closest candle. The clear glass surrounding it felt unnaturally cold, but I didn't hold it for long. I smashed it to the floor before Danny could finish. Pain raked up my right arm as the skulls whipped in my direction and collectively opened their jaws.

A chorus of haunting screams echoed from all directions. "Holy *shit*!" Taran yelled, falling to the floor and taking Shayna and Emme with her. Their heads jerked around to each of the bleating skulls, their faces blanching to white when the skulls shrieked louder.

The cries slowly dwindled. I remained cemented in place, dripping blood from a gash along my right arm, and trying not to wet my pants. Taran's "Holy shit" didn't quite sum up the level of super-suckdom we were in.

"Uh, was that the skulls I heard shrieking?" Danny asked. His voice quivered and he wasn't even in the damn room.

"Yup." I continued to gape, waiting for them to attack.

"That's unfortunate . . . and disturbing."

"Yup." Panty-wetting terror apparently made me quite articulate.

"The good thing is they can't hurt you—they only vocalize their displeasure. However, it says here the power of the bind will probably scratch your flesh."

I examined my arm before glancing back at my sisters. "Danny, this isn't a scratch. The cut I have after smashing just one candle is deep."

"Jesus," he said. "I wasn't expecting this."

At least sixty candles awaited us. Another hunk of Celia-esque dead person fell. "No. But Griselda prepared all the same. Look, this is obviously going to be painful and bloody. Can I do the majority of the smashing?"

My sisters tensed, waiting while Danny flipped through more pages. "I'm sorry, sweetie. It doesn't appear so, since the bind links all of you. While the candles don't have to be destroyed in equal parts, the book states you must each take an active role in the altar's destruction." I heard him pacing. "Had the candles been red, or any other color—or even if there had been a simpler altar—you wouldn't be dealing with any of this."

The soft flickering light continued to mock me, spilling its ugly glow and reminding me of the person who had so cruelly and strategically planned our suffering, and that of our parents. If Griselda was alive, I would have killed her without hesitation and without regret. "The spell protecting the altar is strong, Danny. It could easily sever a vein or artery."

"Then don't do it. Just come back."

Taran raised her hand. "Hold up. As we know, Emme's healing sucks balls—no offense, baby girl." She ignored Emme's blush and continued. "But if we do this, she'll have full control of her healing, right? If so, then she'll fix us after we bust this shit up."

"In theory, yes."

"Then screw it."

"It really hurts," I warned.

Taran beat back the emotion that momentarily crumpled her perfect face. "I think we've been dealt enough pain to handle this, don't you?" She shrugged. "Besides, anything we feel is temporary. The bind's permanent and so is his dad's fate if we stand here like losers and do nothing."

Shayna lifted her battle-ax from where she'd dropped it and edged her way to the opposite side of the circle, cringing when a few toes dropped like chunks of wet snow from the ceiling. She shook off the willies and readied the battle-ax to swing. "Let's do it then. What the heck are we waiting for?"

The rest of us spread out around the circle. "On the count of three, okay? Push past the pain, no matter how bad it gets—the faster we are, the quicker it ends." I crouched and gripped two candles at once; and so did Taran. Emme levitated four from the floor. Shayna swung her hips like a batter ready to save the game. "One. Two. *Three!*"

Griselda deserved to burn in hell.

The harder I smashed, the worse the pain. What felt like serrated knives stabbed through and across my arms, filleting my skin in layers and spilling my blood. I grunted from the burn and the horrific impression of my skin peeling away.

And still I refused to pause.

Despite my sisters' blatant anguish, and how the skulls' eerie shrieks cackled above us, I moved forward—blinking away the tears and noise disorienting me.

Deep within me, my tigress roared—encouraging me as if she knew only my human side could save us. *Lift and destroy. Lift and destroy.* The words became my mantra until lightning crashed and the world exploded in fire.

No . . . not the world—*Taran.*

$$C\text{hapter Seven}$$

Torrents of blue and white flame shot from Taran's hands, striking each bleating skull, and silencing them as they erupted in mini-bombs of shattering bone. She rose from her kneeling position, her bleached white eyes glowing, and panted hard as blood dripped from the slices on her arms. I lurched to her, thinking she was in shock until the corners of her lips curved into a wicked "F-U" smile.

Only one shrieking skull escaped her fury. It bounced along the floor, clicking and clacking its jaw open and shut, audibly conveying its displeasure in the form of disturbing howls.

Shayna made sure the wicked thing didn't make it out the door.

She split the base of her battle-ax like melting silver, converting the small section into a deadly spike by the time she raised it above her head. I didn't see her launch it; the motion was too quick even for my sharpening vision. I only saw it puncture the bone between the skull's eye sockets and stake it to the wall, deadening the last of the horrid cries.

Shayna's bloody shoulders shook as the first of her crazed giggles broke through the tension. "Heh-heh. I nailed a skull to a wall. Hee-hee. I've got aim. I've got mad skills. Ha. Look at me go. Ha-ha-ha."

Taran flipped off the mound of broken glass from the destroyed altar with two very enthusiastic middle fingers. "How do you like us now, *bitch*!"

I grinned at my sisters, pleased and proud of their efforts, and grateful our gashes weren't as severe as the hideous torment had suggested. We looked like we'd fallen into an acre of cacti with an army of rabid cats, but fortunately none of the slices appeared life-threatening.

My smile faded when I caught Emme's stoic expression. Glass crunched beneath her sneakers as she moved across the demolished altar in a trancelike state, tears dripping from her jaw and her body encased with her light.

"Emme?"

She didn't respond and placed herself between Taran and Shayna, bowing her head as she simultaneously clasped their wrists. My other two sisters tensed, waiting for the inevitable pain that accompanied Emme's healing and obviously confused by her despondent state.

Shayna's giggles dwindled into choked sobs as Emme's pale yellow glow enveloped all three. *"Oh,"* she gasped.

Taran used her free hand to cup it over her mouth as the first of her tears began. They stood united, all three shaking from the rush of emotions encompassing their small frames. I should've run to them. My tigress should've growled. But something warned me not to move—they needed Emme's *touch*, and everything else her power was granting them. So, I watched motionless as their cuts sealed, their blood dried, and their soft weeping engulfed the room.

Emme wasn't just healing them.

She was cleansing their souls.

The atmosphere shifted with the growing expanse of Emme's radiance, combating the darkness and sin veiling the room. The plastic bags peeled from the windows, falling almost soundlessly against the dusty floor.

I stole a glance at the ceiling. The semblance of the dead me was gone. Only spider webs claimed the grimy rafters. And despite the vestiges of the skulls and broken glass from the candles, the garage became just another garage.

I couldn't be certain if Emme's power had purified the air and warded away the iniquity, but my instincts told me it had. After all, despite the darkness that had haunted our lives, Emme had faithfully remained our light.

She released my sisters, who continued to openly weep through their grateful smiles. Taran wiped her dirty cheeks with the back of her hand, her eyes resuming their beautiful shade of blue. "Jesus, Emme," she said. "How the hell did you do that?"

"I'm not sure. I just knew I could." Emme's focus remained on me as she left my sisters, her hands extended, and her glow illuminated the darkness. "It's your turn, Celia. Are you ready?"

My jaw tightened. "No. I'm okay the way that I am."

Emme's soft smile faltered. "You're not." She glanced back at Taran and Shayna. "None of us are, or were. Too much has happened."

I stepped out of her reach and attempted to soften my hardening expression. "I'm well enough."

"Dude." Shayna rushed around the thicker patches of broken glass. "It's okay. Don't be afraid. You'll still be you. I promise."

"I don't want to."

Taran stomped through the shattered glass, kicking pieces behind her. "You don't feel different, do you? You didn't feel that charge that the rest of us did?"

I knitted my brows. "What charge?"

"The feeling of freedom that accompanied the severed bind." She swore. "Celia, the only thing keeping you from embracing your full power is you. For shit's sake, let Emme help you through this last step so we can help Danny!"

I stepped back again. "My vision is sharper—"

Taran threw her hands in the air. "I don't give a damn. That's not good enough and you damn well know it!"

"You used 'damn' twice," Shayna pointed out, only to sigh at Taran's glare. "I'm just sayin' you're usually more creative with your language than that, T."

I held out my palm when Taran approached again. "Look, maybe this is as good as it gets for me, you know? Maybe I'm as powerful as I can be."

Taran crossed her arms and glowered, her way of telling me no way in hell was I going to win this debate. "If that's the case, it shouldn't matter what Emme does to you, huh, girlfriend?"

"Well . . . no—but what if it has a bad effect? Danny didn't say anything about needing Emme to heal me."

Danny, who hadn't said a word, chose this moment to speak through Emme's iPhone. "These old magical testaments don't always spell everything out. I think you should try, sweetie. Nothing Emme will do should hurt, especially now that the altar has been destroyed."

"Please don't be afraid, Celia." Emme withdrew some of her power to appear less threatening. "I would never risk your well-being."

I stood my ground. "But what if I hurt you? What if instead of gaining control of my beast, your *touch* is the key that unlocks the cage I house her in?"

"I don't think it is, Celia." Emme's attention flickered to our sisters and back to me again. "In fact, I'm certain of it."

I teetered back and forth, unsure. Fear gripped me like a vise. I didn't want to change who I was. A different me could hurt my family.

"Please, Ceel," Shayna pleaded. "Let's finish what we came for. Time's up, dude!"

Their faces implored me to listen. Well, except for Taran's. Her narrowing glare informed me I needed to just shut up and deal. None of them understood my fear. I verbalized the trepidation holding me back. "Fine. But if something goes wrong, stop me from hurting anyone, any way you can."

My sisters stilled. They knew I was asking them to kill me if I lost control. I wasn't exaggerating. I knew what my beast was capable of. I only hoped they understood as well, and that they would end my life if necessary.

Taran unraveled her arms. Mini-streams of blue and white fire danced along her fingertips as she positioned herself on my left. Shayna took my right as she converted her battle-ax back into a bat. Great. Her strategy included bashing my head in. At Taran's nod, Emme closed in and reached out.

My breath immediately caught. Like the dead leaves of an oak pummeled with a rush of wind, my most deeply repressed feelings were plucked away. At first my defenses fought back, refusing Emme's *touch*. Yet Emme wouldn't falter. She used her power to gently pry through my emotional barricades until she reached into my soul.

The first of my tears released at the memory of my parents' murder. Once again, I watched the last beats of their hearts spill their blood. The memory was too powerful for me to squelch my sob, but as it released, so did a rush of pain.

Emme reached in further, and clenched me within her magic. She meant to help me, but then something changed.

My back abruptly bowed, my spine cracking like something out of a chiropractor's wet dream. That earned me another "Holy shit" from Taran. Emme screamed and yanked her hands from mine. Through my muddled mind I could sense her light cocooning me and levitating me from the floor. My tigress licked her chops excitedly and propelled through my sternum, severing our connection. I tried to tilt my head to see where she'd gone. She'd never left me before. Through my haze, I caught her prancing around the room like freaking Bambi.

My sisters screamed louder. Taran's hysteria made her especially vocal. "Put her back in. Put her back in *now*. Goddamn it, Emme—get her tigress back in 'er!"

"I-I-I don't think I can."

"Omigod, omigod. She's looking at us." Shayna's panic boosted her voice several octaves higher. "Why is she looking at—omigod, she's gonna *eat* us!"

Their voices morphed into distant whispers while the most painful of my memories swirled like a windstorm and demanded my attention. My sobs released harder, raw at first, and violent enough to jerk my body. But with each ragged breath, the brunt of my memories left me.

Relief washed over me with each drop of my tears. To say I'd never again hurt from my past would be a lie. I knew the memories would always haunt me. But I hadn't realized the depth of my emotional wounds until Emme's power reduced them to mending scars.

Time slowed as my body twirled in the air like a petal falling from a rose. I opened my heavy lids after what seemed like forever to find my cuts healed and my golden tigress sitting with her back to me. Her tail flickered from side to side as she examined my sisters with amused interest. Smooth blond-and-white-striped fur draped close to four hundred pounds of lean muscle. Although I'd felt her presence stirring within me for years, I'd never really seen her until that moment. My God, she was beautiful. I could have stared at her for hours.

My poor sisters, conversely, weren't exactly awed by my beast. They huddled in the corner, clutching each other. I tried not to laugh. So much for stopping me at all costs.

My tigress glanced over her shoulder at me as my feet touched down and Emme's residual glow faded. The beast tilted her head as if gauging whether I was ready for her. I was. It may have been minutes or moments since she'd left me, but they were minutes and moments too long. I smiled, my eyes watering. For the first time since she'd birthed within me, I accepted her. I wanted and needed her with me.

"Here, kitty-kitty."

She shared the same olive eyes as me. I guess we were more alike than I'd ever given her credit for. That familiar stare widened when I called her to me. She was happy that I wanted her back. In one graceful leap, she pounced with front paws extended and tackled me against the concrete.

My sisters screamed as I was slammed backward. I lost my breath from the strike and from my tigress's soul merging with mine. My body convulsed violently, riled by the unfathomable boost of her power. Energy fired through every nerve, every synapse of my sprawled and bewildered form, causing one hell of a roar to rip through my throat.

The windows and garage door rattled, sending my sisters into full-out panic. "Shit, shit, shit. Emme, heal her!"

"I can't touch her, she's seizing!"

"Just do it!"

Emme gripped my shoulders as my body melted *into* the floor.

Oh, my God!

I couldn't see. I couldn't hear. I couldn't smell.

I tried to flail my arms, but I no longer possessed them. My body broke into a billion minute particles. Like sand passing through a colander, what remained of me slid through the heavily packed earth. Thank heavens, my tigress shoved past my alarm and took control. Instinctively she stopped our descent into the ground and lurched us up and across.

Just when I thought I would die of asphyxiation, I broke through the soil. I spit out the dirt clogging my mouth while my hands swiped at my eyes, trying to clear the grit out so I could see where the hell I was. My body remained buried in the earth from the waist down. I'd appeared in the yard next to a row of scraggly bushes, a few feet from the old garage.

And I wasn't alone.

Emme's filthy and stunned face met mine and her grip on my shoulders tightened. She screamed— holy hotness, did she scream! — alerting Taran and Shayna to our whereabouts. They raced outside, and joined Emme in voicing their terror.

"Stop!" I yelled over their shrieks. "You're hurting my ears!" Good grief. My supersized hearing had at least doubled in acuity.

Emme panted against me, mud oozing from her mouth and chunks of dirt falling from her hair. "Wh-what was that?"

Taran and Shayna didn't wait for an explanation. Taran reached beneath my arms while Shayna took hold of Emme. They tried to haul us upward, only to knock heads. "Son of a *bitch*."

My tigress nudged me, directing me once more. "Wait, I think I can get us out," I said. "Hang on to me, Emme."

She clutched me as if we dangled from a cliff. I held my breath, and concentrated on forcing my body upward. Well, seems like I concentrated a little too hard. Emme and I were flung from the soil and toppled onto the grass. We rolled off each other in opposite directions, both of us breathing hard.

Shayna loomed over us. "Ceel . . . did you just *travel* underground?"

I swatted more dirt from my eyes. "I think so."

"Like a gopher, Ceel?"

I thought back to how every bit of me and Emme had dissolved into minute particles. "Um. No. Not exactly."

Emme turned her head in my direction. "We shifted like, like, flour."

I examined my hands, grateful my fingers seemed to be in the right place. "I guess that's a good way to describe it."

Emme rose on wobbly legs with her palms out, wary of the ground as if it might swallow her whole. She patted the back of her shorts. "Oh, no, I think I lost my phone in our . . . travels." She peered at the patch of overgrown weeds we'd emerged from. Aside from being flattened, the section appeared undisturbed. "What else do you think you can do?"

I pushed up on my elbows. Dirt smeared every inch of me. "I don't know. I'm almost afraid to find out."

"No shit," Taran muttered. She stared at her hands where mini-bolts of lightning sizzled from her fingertips. "Girlfriends, this could be really good or really, really bad."

Okay. That was new. I stood, mesmerized by all her sparks, when the gate to the yard squeaked. Nieve stood there, watching us quietly. A single tear fell from her eyes. She nodded once as if satisfied and then ran for all she was worth. I raced after her. "Nieve, wait!"

As fast as my tigress moved us, I just barely caught her disappearing around the block. My sisters staggered to a halt behind me. "How did she . . ."

My stare narrowed. "I don't know, Shayna. But she's headed back toward the neighborhood we found her in. We can't let her get away."

The new me could have caught her, but although my sisters possessed heightened power, no way would my tigress and I chance abandoning them. So, we jogged along as fast my sisters' pace allowed until we reached the apartment complex that we'd searched earlier.

My tigress was sure we could find her by scent. But there was no trail to pick up. For the first time, it occurred to me that I hadn't caught even a trace of Nieve's aroma. The realization unnerved me. Everyone and everything carried a scent as unique as their being.

Except Nieve . . .

"She doesn't carry a scent," I said aloud.

Taran's head jerked in my direction. "What the hell does that mean? I thought you said every living thing has one."

"They do."

Emme slowed to a stop, breathing hard from the run. "Could it be that she's in league with Griselda?"

I attempted to dust off the dirt coating my arms. "If she was, she wouldn't have led us to the altar."

Taran glared. "Unless she thought it would kill us."

"I don't think so. My tigress gets pissy around people she perceives as a threat. She didn't with Nieve. Come to think of it, she didn't even react."

Shayna tapped her bat against her palm. "Unless she didn't realize she was there. If she couldn't sniff her, maybe she couldn't see her either."

My beast stirred within me, riled by my sisters' suspicions. I soothed her back into quiescence, surprised by how easily and well she responded to my efforts. "Look, I'm not sure what's happening. But we need to find out—especially if Nieve can somehow prevent us from helping Danny. Come on, we need to hurry."

Emme gripped my wrist before I could step onto the old stoop. "Wait. If you can't smell her, how do you know which way to go?"

My head involuntarily wrenched up and I found myself gazing at the upper stories of the battered old apartment building. "I don't know. But something is luring me this way. Let's just hope we don't have to kill it."

We climbed three flights of steps and cut right, into a long hall of closed doors. I continued forward, passing each one until I reached the last door. Before I knocked, I knew we were in the right place. I could sense Nieve's presence, although I couldn't exactly tell how. I rapped my knuckles against the splintering brown door and stepped away from the threshold, just in case someone answered with a spray of bullets. Yeah, I'd seen my share of crime shows.

"Who's there?" an old woman croaked in Spanish.

I motioned to Emme, knowing her voice would sound the least threatening. "Pardon me, ma'am. Is Nieve home?" she asked in the same language.

There was a brief pause. "You know my granddaughter?"

Emme glanced at us before answering. "Um, yes. From, um, school."

The door creaked open and a woman dressed all in black answered the door. I wasn't tall by any means, but I absolutely towered over her hunched form. Cataracts dulled her soft brown eyes. It was a wonder the poor woman could see at all. She motioned us forward. "Welcome, dear ones. I'm sure she'd like the company."

Taran and I exchanged stares before I took my first step forward. Roaches scurried along the battered wood floor as we slowly crossed the small alcove. A tiny kitchen was crammed against the wall on the left, and what appeared to be a small bedroom lay directly ahead.

But I barely noticed anything past that, too stunned to move when I caught sight of Nieve.

She lay semi-reclining in an old metal hospital bed with her long braids draped over her bony shoulders, dressed in the same stained pink shirt we'd seen her in just minutes ago. The nasal cannula taped against her sunken cheeks whistled with the oxygen futilely trying to ease her short, pained breaths, and thick white fluid from an IV dripped into a vein in her left arm.

Nieve didn't acknowledge our presence. Then again, how could she? She was barely alive.

The old woman gave us her back and shuffled to her kitchen, oblivious to our stupefied expressions. She poured soup into a bowl and then returned with it and sat beside Nieve. With her free hand she placed a dish towel over Nieve's chest, as best as her arthritic and swollen fingers would allow. "I'm not very good at feeding her," she admitted, her wrinkles etched with sadness.

Emme closed in, taking in Nieve's emaciated form with eyes that brimmed with impending tears. "I-I'm so sorry. We didn't realize she was sick." She placed her small hand over Nieve's forehead and called forth her *touch*. Nieve's grandmother glanced up, confused by the source of the light. She stood and went to the windows, tugging the drapes closed.

Emme withdrew her *touch* as the woman returned to the bed. She shook her head at us. Her power failed to have an effect on Nieve's condition. That wasn't a big surprise. Emme could only heal injuries, not illnesses. The sudden boost in her power didn't seem to have changed that. "How long does Nieve have?" she asked the old woman.

Taran and Shayna gasped, surprised by Emme's bluntness. But my little sister's hospice training told her death wasn't far from finding Nieve. Her grandmother didn't answer, but her quivering lip was enough of a response. So were the tears that glazed her opaque stare.

I didn't argue or attempt to offer hope. I knew Emme was right. While I'd failed to pick up Nieve's scent before, I could smell her now. Her scent of drying autumn leaves was unmistakable. So was the aroma of life leaving her body. Nieve's lungs would soon take their last agonized breath. And there wasn't a damn thing any of us could do about it.

"Why?" Shayna clutched her bat tight, trying not to cry. "Why is she like this?"

Nieve's grandmother poured a bit of soup from a spoon into Nieve's mouth. Most of the broth dribbled down Nieve's slack jaw and onto her neck. The woman wiped Nieve's skin with the towel, her crackling voice hoarse with regret. "Because bad things happen to good girls who stand against the dark ones."

<h1 style="text-align:center">Chapter Eight</h1>

We gave Nieve's grandmother every last dime in our pockets and silently whispered our thanks to the cousin we'd found too late in life. We didn't speak again until we returned to our car. As much as we wanted to stay, we couldn't help her. But we could still help Danny.

The people gathered near our sedan quickly scattered. Dirty, blood-smeared women, I supposed, had that effect on them.

I hurried around to the opposite side and yanked open the rear door. "Shayna, text Danny and let him know we're on our way."

She whipped out her phone from her pocket and buckled herself in before sending the text. Taran peeled away from the curve and toward the back roads leading to Route 22. "Okay, this whole thing wasn't batshit crazy or anything."

"No, not at all," I muttered.

Taran stopped at the light. "What I don't get is if Nieve's half-dead, then what the hell were we talking to?"

I shrugged and stretched out in the backseat, suddenly unbearably tired despite the anxiety racing through my bloodstream. "Near as I can figure, I think it's a fragment of what remains of her."

Shayna turned around from the passenger seat to face me. "Do you think we can help her? I mean, she helped us and she wasn't even, like, totally real."

Emme played with her palms. "I don't think anything can help her, Shayna. From what I can tell, she has a week at most. I'm surprised she's held on this long."

I leaned my head back, trying to get comfortable. My unease at finding Nieve in her ailing state and my anxiety over the fight we still faced with the vamps made it impossible. "She seemed so thin when we saw her. But I never would have guessed her condition was related to illness—or whatever has caused her slow death."

"You mean *who*ever." Taran peered at me through the rearview mirror. "You know Griselda or her hell spawn did this to her. Nieve admitted as much when we spoke to her—so did her grandmother."

"I think you're right. If she had more time, maybe we could . . ."

My voice trailed off at the sight of the misery edging its way along Emme's gentle features. "She doesn't have the time we would need, Celia."

Yeah. And neither did Mr. Matagrano.

All was quiet except for the hum of the tires against the road and the rock ballad playing on low volume through the speakers. "You know what I think?"

Shayna said after a while. "I think Nieve's been waiting for us to come along." She smiled softly at Taran's quizzical stare. "It's not such a crazy thought, T, when you consider how she came to us."

Taran focused on the road. "Maybe. Maybe not. But like Emme said, there's nothing we can do for her now. God willing, the poor thing will find her peace soon. In the meantime, the goddamn night isn't over yet."

"It's sure not." I leaned my head against the glass, trying to figure out a way to find Danny's dad. The locating spell wouldn't work without Mr. Matagrano's fresh blood. And the poor man probably had none to spare with Giovanna . . .

My eyes closed without permission. I hadn't expected to doze, much less dream. But I did.

I walked through a white haze as a soft breeze swept my long hair against my bare breasts and shoulders. Despite my toned muscles and flat stomach, I hated being naked. Nakedness represented vulnerability.

And I refused to be vulnerable.

But there, wherever there was, wasn't a place to fear. The sense of peace and safety that drifted with each soft caress of the breeze lulled my fears and assured me that I was protected. I thought I was alone until the hulking form of a tall male stepped through the thickening haze.

My eyes widened, but they didn't help me see. This man wasn't really a man, he was more like a shadow, if shadows could manifest into a physical form. He chuckled and spoke in a deep-timbred voice intermixed with soft, gruff growls. "So, you found a way to let me in, little tigress."

"Huh?"

I stepped away as he advanced, but my actions didn't dissuade him. He smiled. Or I thought he did. Crap, what exactly was happening here?

"Don't you know me, Celia?" he asked.

"No."

I didn't see him move, I just felt a strong arm gently circle my waist while a large hand passed through my hair to skim along my bare back. Soft lips swept along my jawline. "Are you sure you don't know me?" he rumbled.

In my reality, I would have shoved him away, but not before I snapped off at least one of his wandering hands. But every stroke, every whisper of his warm breath, soothed and enticed me. My lids fluttered. "Oh, no . . . I'd remember you . . ."

His heartbeat pounded against my breasts, reassuring me with each rhythmic drum. This was right—no, *he* was right.

Somewhere deep within my mind, I recognized this male as another preternatural. One that wasn't a part of me, but one I had no desire to abandon. Perhaps he was the start of REM sleep—a developing dream or fantasy of what I really needed in a man. Or maybe, just maybe, he was real.

His lips passed over mine. "Do you know me now, Celia?"

Rock-hard muscles passed beneath my palms as my hands slid along the silky skin of his broad chest. "Hmm?" I managed.

He nuzzled my neck, laughing once more. "I asked if you knew me."

"No," I groaned. "But I really want to . . ."

"Celia, *Celia!*"

I startled awake, pissed as all hell my dream was interrupted. *"What?"*

My sisters blinked back at me from their seats. Emme dropped her hand from my shoulder. It took me several seconds to realize we were parked in our driveway. "Are you okay, honey? You were making strange sounds and weren't waking up."

Strange sounds? Oh, *God.* Had I been that vocal during the best pretend make-out moment of my life? Based on my sisters' shocked expressions, I had. "Um . . . I'm just hungry. It's been a while since I've, you know, eaten."

A wicked smile spread across Taran's face. "That's not what it sounded like to me."

Shayna angled her chin. "Yeah, and why the heck were you touching yourself like that?"

I jerked my hands from my breasts "Uh . . ."

Taran busted out laughing as Danny hurried out of the house, practically falling in his haste to reach us. He banged on the window, even though we were staring straight at him. "Quennel called. He found my dad!"

We rushed to strip out of our blood-caked clothes and into old worn clothes we could risk being re-bloodied in. To my surprise, Emme's newfound *touch* had healed even my old scars. My butt was whole once more. Yippee. Too bad I likely only had more wounds to look forward to.

Shayna drove us in Danny's truck. Now, we typically didn't allow Shayna to drive anyone, in anything, anywhere. The tri-state area was packed with crazy road-rage drivers ready to smash into anyone who cut—or flipped—them off.

These same drivers were scared shitless of Shayna.

Case in point, she stomped on the accelerator almost the entire way to the Jersey Shore. "Brakes are for pussies" was Shayna's unspoken motto. Her idea of slowing was releasing the gas pedal just enough to serpent around any cars ahead. No one passed Shayna, ever. And no cop could give her a ticket while Taran's influence was around.

Since it was past midnight and Labor Day was now long gone, there were few cars on the parkway to compete with Shayna's might. She laughed like the *Looney Tunes* witch chasing Bugs Bunny on her broom as she barreled through the night. No curve was too sharp, no speed too high. Shayna was a woman possessed by the ghosts of Indy racers past.

Damn those evil ghouls.

I gripped the armrest and kept my eyes glued shut. "What's the plan, exactly?"

Danny screamed briefly as Shayna cut a sharp left, then an immediate right, then straightened the wheel. He'd made the mistake of opening his eyes when he tried to answer. His bad. I assured him she'd tell us when we reached Sandy Hook.

His voice trembled. "Quennel didn't really say. He said to get to the fishing side of the beach. And that my father was there."

"Giovanna must be either crazier or ballsier than we thought," Taran muttered. "That's not far from where the U.S. Coast Guard has their base. Why the hell would she risk drawing national attention to herself?"

"Probably because she has an army of vamps that can influence the minds of anyone who arrives." I thought more about it. "And because she's nuttier than a truckload of cashews."

Danny attempted to slow his breathing when Shayna veered the truck hard enough to ram poor Emme's head into my shoulder. "Giovanna supposedly has a place in Spring Lake," he said. "Quennel found an informant, uh, willing to divulge her location."

Or not so willing. "If Quennel knows she's in Spring Lake, he's already there. Why hasn't he texted you to tell us what's happening?"

"I don't know, Celia. But like he admitted to us, he's out for himself—he wants to achieve his own place among the masters. I doubt he'll help us any more than he has."

Shayna ceased her wicked cackles just long enough to speak. "No worries, dude. We're here."

I tucked Emme against me as we skidded to a harrowing stop. It was the only instance Shayna had used the brakes from the moment we jetted out of our driveway until now. My tigress rumbled, alert and ready to charge. Me? Not so much. I staggered out of the truck and into the brisk night, my brain and stomach continuing to lurch forward despite my steadfast position.

Shayna skipped out of the vehicle, twirling her wrist until her faithful bat transformed into a lethal sword. She needed a weapon when Taran crashed out of the truck and onto her knees, scraping her legs on the asphalt. "Son of a *bitch*. Who was the asshat who deemed you worthy of a license? There's something goddamn wrong with you!"

Emme would've healed the scrapes soaking blood through Taran's jeans if she wasn't retching over a railing in the abandoned parking lot. I wasn't sure why Shayna had chosen this location to dump us in, until I took in my surroundings. Holy hotness, by pure strategy or possibly dumb luck, this area was closest to the Coast Guard station. And all the action. "Danny, come here."

He used the door to ease himself out and steadied himself against the hood. "What is it, Celia? What do you see?"

I stayed low and headed to the far corner while the sea roared like a beast and waves crashed along the beaten shore. The only streetlight blinked on the opposite side, far from where Shayna had careened us to a stop. Clouds covered most of the quarter moon's glow, hiding Danny's truck in darkness. "Look over there, near the dock."

One by one the others joined me. "Near the bonfire?" Danny asked. He blinked several times and adjusted his glasses. "Celia, I can barely see the dock. And if it wasn't for the light of the fire, I wouldn't even be able to make that out."

My tigress licked her paws within me, feigning indifference, but I knew better. She was giving me a taste of our new heightened senses. *Okay, kitty, try not to get so full of yourself.* "There're about twenty vamps." I squinted. "Uh, naked and dancing around the fire. Wait, no, they're wearing fig leaves around their, you know, manhoods."

Taran laughed, despite herself. "Did you just say 'manhoods'? What the hell, Celia? Can't you just say co—"

"Taran!" Emme admonished. She surrounded Taran with her healing light. More to distract than heal, I imagined.

I leaned forward, my tigress growling, when the men stopped dancing. A woman dressed in a sheer gown appeared; her white-blond hair was woven into multiple braids and she was leading a portly man in boxers on a leash. The man collapsed to his knees, then fell face-first into the sand, unmoving.

"Oh, God, Danny. That's your dad."

Chapter Nine

Danny swung his leg over the railing. I clasped his arm and hauled him back. "Wait. We can't just rush in."

"Is he all right? Did he look okay?"

I held tight to his arm. "He just collapsed in the sand."

Danny went perfectly still. "Is he . . . ?"

I peered out, but couldn't bring myself to tell him what I saw. The female, Giovanna I presumed, straddled Mr. Matagrano, bouncing up and down on his butt while holding the leash taut. She lifted his head from the sand, but the stupid bitch didn't know, or care, enough that she was strangling him.

Another vamp bent to speak with her. She didn't like what he had to say. She released Mr. Matagrano and smacked the vamp hard across the face. The force of the blow sent the leech reeling, with blood streaming from his mouth.

Two more vamps approached her slowly with their palms out as she once more reached for the leash.

She giggled at something the taller vamp with red hair said and allowed him to lift her from Danny's father. The other vamp nudged Danny's father with his foot. I thought I heard a groan, but I couldn't be sure. When the vamp lifted Mr. Matagrano's lifeless form over his shoulder, I knew we had to move.

"Celia, what's happening?"

Danny was brilliant. I needed his mind, and couldn't allow panic to cloud his judgment. But I couldn't censor what had transpired. "Look, I don't know where Quennel is or if he's even coming. He hasn't returned your calls or answered your texts since first telling you where to find your dad."

The muscles in Danny's shoulders tensed. "Do you think he set us up?"

"I don't know, Danny. What I do know is your dad is barely breathing. We have to move now."

I leaped from the elevated lot and landed in a deep crouch in the sand, perfectly poised and ready to haul tail across the beach.

Until my sisters and Danny landed in a heap on top of me and I ate about half a cup of sand.

They rolled off me, moaning while I coughed out the nasty stuff. I scraped the excess with my nails while drooling like a dumbass.

"Oops. Sorry, Celia," Emme mumbled.

"What the hell was that?"

Everyone staggered to their feet. Emme covered her face. "I thought I could lift everyone with my *force*. But I guess my aim is just as bad as always."

I stood and lowered her hands away from her face. "Look, this is no time to try out our powers on each other, but it is time to hit and hit hard. Shayna, you stab, slice, or behead anything that gets in your way. Taran, you burn or electrocute things to cinders—I don't care how. Emme, you toss everyone out of Danny's way so he can get to his dad." I locked eyes with Danny. "Get him back to the truck. If you don't have a clear way back to us, get to the Coast Guard station. Honk the horn, smash into the fence, make a lot of noise. Do you hear me? There are twenty vamps. We can't take them on alone."

Taran gave me a hard stare. "What are you going to do, Celia?"

I yanked off my sweatshirt and shorts. "Me? Consider me the first line of a very strong offense—*shit, Danny, could you turn around!*"

He whirled to the side. "Sorry, sweetie."

My bra and panties hit the sand and so did four hundred pounds of raging feline.

The vamps had probably prepared for a great deal.

But I was betting they hadn't prepared for me.

The sweeping sound of sand being kicked up by my paws was the only noise I made as I raced along the beach, yet even that subtle disturbance was muffled by the sea's increasing turmoil. My stare honed in on Giovanna's neck and my fangs moistened with the thought of digging them into her flesh. I wasn't afraid to let my tigress out this time. She needed to be here.

My paws dug deeper into the sand, propelling me further toward my target. I knew Giovanna's keep would try to protect her. Just as I knew they'd try to kill me. But all I needed to do was buy my family time to rush in, and give Danny the opportunity to save his father.

Giovanna didn't look my way. She was too busy twirling around in some kind of bizarre dance. Her sheer pink nightgown fluttered around her as she stopped spinning just to thrust her chest up toward the dwindling moonlight. I almost felt sorry about how hard I tackled her.

Well. Not really.

My weight struck her hard enough to plow a deep ridge into the sand. We stopped several yards away, her stunned face staring at me before her furious hiss sent her family charging. Something heavy pounced on me before my tigress *shifted* all three of us beneath the sand. I surfaced further down the beach alone. Giovanna and the vamp who'd tackled me hadn't clung to me like Emme had. I left both buried deep within the sand.

A pair of bare feet wiggled above the surface. The hairy ankles told me they didn't belong to Giovanna. That meant girlfriend was somewhere *way* down under. One vamp yanked at the feet uselessly while his buddies circled the surrounding area. I hid behind a small cluster of boulders, watching them and waiting to act. The vamps scratched their heads, befuddled as to where their mistress had gone. A blond swore. I recognized him as the James Dean vamp I'd nearly castrated.

My family and Danny inched toward us. Although I'd given them time, they still weren't anywhere near me. I cringed, watching their sad lack of athleticism in action. They stumbled to a stop, pausing to catch their breaths, then continued forward in pathetically awkward jogging motions. What sucked was their wheezing and pants were loud enough to attract the vamps, who snarled and raced toward them with their fangs and deadly nails out.

I pounced on the closest vamp to me and dragged him away by his throat. Each clench of my jaws brought on another of his gargled screams. I growled, shaking him hard to draw attention away from my family. James Dean and the vamps froze. Whether by scent or instinct, James recognized me instantly. His furrowed glare promised me pain. "Split up and take them out, now!" he told the others.

The vamp's vertebra snapped beneath my jowls before he exploded into a pile of ash. Two vamps tackled me and another launched himself in the air, only to ignite as a bolt of blue and white lightning nailed him in the back.

Taran!

The vamps on top of me slashed me with their nails, eager to kill me fast. They raked at my skin while I swatted back with my front and back claws. My opponents were strong and knew how to fight. I couldn't kick them off me. I could only claw at their flesh and snap my fangs, moving fast and trying to shield my heart.

One had just gripped my throat when his weight, and his buddy's, abruptly left mine. Emme had arrived and this time her crappy aim worked in her favor. The vamps' skulls crunched against the stack of boulders.

Except they didn't die.

They rose to their feet, wobbling and flailing their arms while searching for their dented heads. With hands-down the worst high-pitched battle cry ever, Shayna appeared, driving her sword through each of their hearts.

Sweat poured down her face. "Sorry it took us so long, Ceel," she panted. "Running in the sand is *hard*."

I licked her hand; just grateful she'd arrived in time—

The earth shook.

It was my only warning before Giovanna jetted from the sand, screeching. Taran launched a giant blue and white fireball, which Giovanna swatted back at her like a ball. It struck Taran in the chest, knocking her down and engulfing her with her own fire.

Shayna and I charged, killing two more vampires before Emme's screams halted our strikes.

One vampire was dragging Danny along in a headlock. His father lay in the sand. He'd barely made it a few yards down the beach. James Dean twisted Emme's wrist behind her back with one hand while the other grasped her throat. Another vamp held Taran. She'd reabsorbed her fire, but her staggering feet told me that no way was she ready to release it.

"Drop your weapon," James Dean told Shayna, making Emme scream by tightening his grip on her wrist.

Shayna did as he asked, and the remaining vampires pounced on us. I don't know how many held me down, but at least one wrenched my fuzzy head up so Giovanna could kick me in the face.

Stars exploded in my vision with each of her kicks. "They tried to take my pet," she whimpered. She kicked again. "They tried to take my baby."

I couldn't focus enough to *shift* myself beneath the sand, and the dizzying blows barely allowed me to keep my beast form. My tigress urged me up. But even the boost of her power couldn't help me. Giovanna cried miserably, accusing us of ruining her party. "We were getting married," she said, motioning wildly to Danny's father.

To make herself feel better, or to make us feel worse, she stripped and resumed her bizarre dance while the vamps sang every last nursery rhyme I knew.

Never again would "Itsy Bitsy Spider" hold the same meaning for me.

Every movement of her arms, every leap in the air, made me think Giovanna was falling deeper into Nutsville. Hell, she should have been the town's damn mayor. Some of the vamps glanced at each other uneasily. They knew their mistress was crazy, but they feared her all the same. Most encouraged her, I suppose to stay in her favor. "Dance, my mistress. Dance! Oh, yes!" James Dean encouraged.

Kiss ass.

I writhed, trying to gain some leverage and enough breath to *shift* myself underground. That earned me several blows to my back from the vamps holding me, forcing what little air I'd retained to leave my lungs with audible wheezes. My jaw snapped when it crashed into the sand. Shit, we were screwed.

The vamps applauded her when she took her final bow. She smiled, delighted, and then approached me. "You like your family, don't you, tiger?"

My entire body tensed and I growled.

Her smile widened. "Drown them. And let her watch."

My sisters kicked wildly. Danny lay draped against the vamp's arms. I jerked my body hard, trying to move enough to breathe. The vamp dragging Taran burst into flames as she surrounded herself with fire. Giovanna laughed and tackled her. She held her face down in the water, laughing as a wave crashed over them.

James Dean winked at me as he dragged Emme into the ocean. "Masters are immune to flame," he said.

I whirled and fought, barely able to breathe. Another wave, this time larger, crashed down, engulfing everyone. The vamps resurfaced, looking around frantically, their arms empty of Danny and my sisters. Giovanna shrieked and propelled herself onto the beach, followed closely by James Dean.

She wrenched Danny's father to her and ran to the dock. I didn't know what was happening until my sisters and Danny shot out of the water with Quennel and his vampires.

Chapter Ten

The vamps loosened their hold at Quennel's appearance, just enough for me to gather enough air to *shift* belowground. This time I yanked them with me. The travel beneath the sand disoriented them. I surfaced and rammed my claws through the chests of two of them and beheaded a third.

My pale sisters spewed seawater near the stack of boulders. Quennel lowered Danny beside Emme and motioned to me. "Come, Celia. We mustn't permit Giovanna's escape."

Quennel's vamps formed a protective arc around my family and friend. Shayna crawled along the sand to retrieve her sword, while the power building within Emme and Taran fired across my fur. They were recovering. And they were furious. They would soon attack. And Quennel's vamps would make sure they weren't alone.

I bolted after Quennel. My sisters would see to Danny's safety, and I needed to see to his father's. I assumed Quennel had a boat waiting at the end of the dock to race after Giovanna's. Her motorboat sped along the waves to a large yacht in the distance. I briefly saw her drape Mr. Matagrano's lifeless form over her shoulder before she climbed the ropes like a black widow.

"Can you swim?" Quennel asked. My widening eyes answered for me. "No? Then I shall help."

Quennel ripped me from the wooden pier when I tried to straddle one of the posts and launched us into the freezing ocean. I flailed with my paws pathetically, and gasped for air as I broke through the relentless waves. Tigers could swim, but they didn't purr. I purred and was damn good at drowning. Just a few of many traits that made me weird.

Quennel made sure I didn't drown. He gripped me beneath my front leg and shot through the water—never taking a breath, but lifting me enough so I could take enough for both of us. My heart pounded, mostly with terror. I wasn't afraid to fight the vamps, but I was afraid to be left to drown.

Waves smacked against my chest as I wrenched my nose upward. Quennel continued forward, moving like a shark against the angry current. Despite the distance, he didn't breathe until we reached the sprawling yacht, gasping when he grasped the lowest rung of the rope ladder. "Go, climb."

I caught the next rung with my human hands when he flung me up. No way could I climb this contraption as a beast. Of course, our arrival had made too much noise. James Dean appeared with a harpoon gun and shot it my way. He missed me when I veered to the side, but managed to strike Quennel in the shoulder.

I yanked on the rope when James tried to pull him, forcing him down to me.

He punched me hard in the face, but his satisfied smirk turned to horror when my claws cracked through his sternum. He met my eyes briefly and exploded into ash. I ascended as fast as I could, with Quennel at my heels. We scrambled onto the deck as three more vamps appeared. Quennel yanked the harpoon from his shoulder and used it to attack. "Go, find your friend's father."

I *changed* back into a tigress and barreled around the yacht until I caught a whiff of Mr. Matagrano . . . and Giovanna. She had him alone. I'd seen what she'd done to him in the presence of others. What was she doing to him now?

I crept down the steps into a large cabin. There on a bed, Giovanna straddled Danny's father as she smacked him in the face. "Tell me I'm beautiful!" she demanded. "Tell me you *love me*!"

My hind legs catapulted me across the room and into her side, knocking the crazy bitch away from him. She kicked me off her, sending me soaring into the opposite wall. I rolled to the floor and onto all fours when Quennel appeared, covered with ash. I thought he'd zing her with some smart remark or insult before attacking. Instead he charged right at her without saying a word. He wanted her to die.

They went blow for blow. Giovanna's age and power fed her lethality. And although Quennel's strength and speed made him a worthy match, he wasn't enough. He needed a tigress on his side.

I sank my fangs into her ankle, snapping the bones as her nails pierced through Quennel's neck. The three of us rolled around, hurtling into every piece of furniture in the room. Quennel and I fought hard, but Giovanna continued to beat us like we mere humans. Despite our combined strength we needed more help.

Help arrived in the form of crazy Brillo hair and stick-thin limbs.

Danny hollered as he drove a knife into Giovanna's heart. Her eyes widened and she paused, giving Quennel time to tear off her head in one brutal pull. With his fist, he pounded Danny's knife further into her heart until all that remained of Giovanna was a mountain of ash.

My body collapsed and I *changed* form again. My human self crawled across the floor and onto the bed where Danny lay with his father.

"Dad. Dad, can you hear me?"

His father groaned, but couldn't speak.

"We need to get him to Emme," I gasped.

Cheers erupted at the door. I jerked as two more vampires hurried in. One embraced Quennel, meeting his lips hard. "You did it, my love," he said.

He and the other vampire led Quennel to the door, allowing my sisters to pass before exiting. Relief washed over their soaking wet and trembling bodies when they saw me, but Taran swore when she caught sight of Danny's father in his debilitated state. "Let's go. Emme can heal him when we're safe."

I gathered the throw blanket at the foot of the bed and wrapped it around me, then helped Danny lift his father.

Quennel smiled when we stepped out. "Forgive our late arrival. It seemed Giovanna used your Coast Guard and the rest of her vampires to keep us busy at her home." His smile softened as he took in Danny and his father. "It is good we both achieved what we wanted, no?"

Danny appeared close to breaking down, but he still managed to speak. "Yes. Thank you." His voice cracked when he acknowledged me and my sisters: "Thank you for helping me."

I tried to keep all my girl parts covered while giving Danny's hand a gentle squeeze. "You're welcome, Danny."

Taran stepped forward. "Look, this has been all shits and giggles, but we really just want to go home." She glanced back at us. "We have new lives to begin."

Quennel motioned to the blond at his side. The blond grinned, flashing a bit of his fang. "I'll take you back to your vehicle."

I exchanged glances with my sisters, unsure whether to trust any of the vampires. Sure, Quennel had helped, but he had something at stake for himself.

Shayna leaned to whisper in my ear. "Blondie brought us to you, Ceel. If the vamps wanted to kill us, they would have already tried."

Point made. I nodded in their direction. "Um, okay. Thanks."

"Jerry," the blond said.

"Thanks, Jerry," I repeated.

The vamps stilled and looked out over the water. A distant roar signaled another high-power yacht's approach. I tensed, worried that more of Giovanna's family had found us. In contrast, the vamps relaxed their shoulders. The edges of Quennel's lover's mouth curved into a smile as he placed his hand over his heart. "The master is coming, Quennel. Do you feel him, dear one?"

Quennel lifted his partner's hand and kissed his knuckles. "Yes, Eloy. He will be pleased, no?"

"Indeed, he will," Eloy said.

"Hell yeah," Jerry chimed in. "You did it, Quennel. You earned your rank among the masters!"

Emme leaned into me. "What's happening, Celia?"

"Their master is approaching."

Shayna's head whipped in the direction of the incoming boat. It was now close enough that they could hear it, too. She snapped the metal clip from her hair and converted it into a dagger. Quennel shook his head. "That won't be necessary, my friends. My master, Angelo Cusamano, will not harm you, I swear it."

He marched to the opposite end of the yacht and fell to his knees in a deep bow. His friends followed suit but remained at our sides. Within seconds, three vampires leaped onto the boat. The one in the center was wearing a silky blue shirt and a charcoal gray suit that hugged an ass I could have chopped veggies on.

"Master," Quennel said. "It pleases me to see you."

Angelo smiled and stroked Quennel's long hair.

Then ripped Quennel's head from his shoulders in one merciless yank.

Everything happened at once. I shoved Danny and my sisters back while vamps on either side of Quennel held his flailing body so their master could dig through his neck and rip out his heart.

My heart thudded painfully against my sternum and my throat clenched tight. That *bastard*. He'd never planned to give Quennel his own domain. He'd sent him to kill Giovanna so he could then rob him of his power.

Jerry wrenched back Quennel's lover, clasping a firm hand over his mouth. "No, Eloy." The blond whispered low and frantically into Eloy's ear. I couldn't hear what he said, but whatever it was kept Eloy in place, even though what remained of his love burst into ash before his eyes.

Eloy choked back a sob and attempted to compose himself. Angelo ignored him to wipe his filthy hands on his slacks. He stepped over Quennel's ashes and approached us, as if he hadn't just murdered one of his family members.

My claws itched to protrude and claw. Angelo smiled confidently. After all, he'd just absorbed the power of two master vamps, why should he fear us? "Ah, and who do we have here?"

Jerry and Eloy stepped forward, keeping their gazes lowered. Jerry, although trembling, did all the talking. "These women and the men are allies of Quennel, master. They helped to defeat Giovanna, which in turn allowed you to inherit her power."

Angelo took another step forward. "But I don't need them anymore, do I?"

My sisters spread out, ready to fight, as six more vampires leaped onto the deck. Jerry stepped in front of us with his hands out. "I beg you not to harm them, master—their leader is a tigress!"

Angelo's head whipped in Jerry's direction. "A *were*?"

It was Eloy's turn to speak up. "She transforms into a tigress, master. I fear for your safety should the *weres* learn she was harmed."

They were implying I was a *were,* without really calling me one. Smart, considering their master and every vamp present would be able to sniff through their lies.

I let the blanket fall to my feet and *changed* form, then prowled around them, licking my chomps as if I couldn't wait to take my next bite. The vamps could probably smell the extent of my trepidation with every breath I took. But I didn't care. My goal was to give the impression that I belonged with the *weres,* even though I wasn't anything like them, and they sure as hell were nothing like me.

Angelo's attention left me to focus on my sisters. "And the others?"

"I don't know what they are, master," Eloy said quietly. "But they are her family. The humans' memories can easily be altered, so do not fear for our discovery."

Doubt shadowed Angelo's sharp features. He didn't fully believe Jerry or Eloy, but he couldn't dismiss the golden tigress stalking around them. "Get them out of my sight," he spat.

Emme reached for my borrowed blanket as Jerry and Eloy ushered my sisters, Danny, and his father to the rear of the boat. The vamps grabbed two at a time and jumped from the edge. I waited until they were all off the yacht, then followed, stopping to glance one last time at Angelo. He met me with a smile laced with sin and challenge. "Until we meet again, little tigress?"

I had to work not to peel back my lips and bare my fangs. Should Angelo and I ever meet again, one of us would bleed. Of this, I was absolutely sure.

"Ceel!" Shayna urged.

I trotted to the stern of the yacht and leaped into the cramped speedboat. I landed as a human and quickly wrapped my body in the blanket Emme held. The boat shot forward, rapidly putting space between us and Angelo.

Emme's soft yellow light encompassed Danny's dad. "He's bruised and has lost a lot of blood, but I think he'll be okay."

Eloy drove the boat in silence as tears streamed down his face. Jerry left him to place his hand on Danny's shoulder as he hovered over his father. "Do you want him to forget?"

Danny rubbed his face hard. He'd lost his glasses and could likely barely focus. But he saw and could sense enough of his father's torment. "Yes. Please. Make him believe he's been sick. And that all *this* has all been a bad dream." He sniffed. "I don't want him remembering what that lunatic did to him."

Jerry nodded and did as he asked. Mr. Matagrano woke abruptly, terror streaking across his beaten face until Jerry's voice lulled him back to sleep. It didn't take Jerry long to influence his mind; Mr. Matagrano's weakened state left him with little energy to fight. When Jerry finished, he turned to Danny. "I'm supposed to change your memory, too." He glanced at each one of us. "And I'd do the same for all of you if I could. But I think it's better that you remember."

We nodded. Some things, however painful, should not be forgotten.

The boat continued along, skimming over the angry-looking waves and into the howling wind. The sun rose above the horizon just as Eloy maneuvered the boat into a dock far from the one we'd departed from. I supposed the vampires didn't want to risk running into their master anytime soon.

We headed down the beach toward Danny's truck. Jerry carried Mr. Matagrano. He said that anyone passing by at this time would be more inclined to accept him carrying a man over his shoulder as opposed to me.

My sisters remained tight-lipped on the long walk. We hadn't known Quennel, not really. And although he'd insisted he was out for himself, he'd helped us and ensured our survival. Now his friends saw to our safety. Maybe all the creatures of the night weren't so bad after all.

We placed Mr. Matagrano in the back of the truck with Danny and Emme. Shayna took the center seat in front after Taran flat-out told her, "If you think we're letting you drive back, you're out of your goddamn mind."

I watched Eloy stare out to sea as his tears continued to draw lines into his beautiful face. My tigress urged me into the truck. My human side had me walking to Eloy. "I'm sorry for your loss," I said. "I know you loved him."

Eloy wiped his eyes and sniffed. "You seem like a good girl, Celia." His face softened when he met mine. "Do yourself and your family a tremendous favor and keep far away from the supernatural world. It is no place for someone with your heart."

He crossed his arms and resumed his grief-stricken posture. Jerry came to stand beside him. Together they stared out across the Atlantic Ocean, mourning for a friend they'd never see again.

I left them to their goodbyes and returned to the truck. Taran stepped on the gas the minute I shut the door.

As we veered onto the parkway, I leaned my head against the glass and thought about how Eloy had referred to me as a "good" girl, despite the viciousness he'd witnessed me unleash. I also thought about Nieve's grandmother's last words to us, "Bad things happen to good girls who stand against the dark ones."

We needed to stay away from the darkness. Me, my sisters, *everyone*. If the last two days had taught us anything, it was that the mystical world was no place for us.

Too bad we couldn't keep away. Too bad we ran into this weird new world full force. Vamps in Jersey were just the beginning of our journey into the supernatural. And hell, that world didn't know what it was in for.

Read on as the Weird Girls saga continues with *Sealed with a Curse,* the first full length novel in The Weird Girls Urban Fantasy Romance series by Cecy Robson. The excerpt has been set for this edition only and may not reflect the final content of the final novel.

Sealed with a Curse

A Weird Girls Novel

By

CECY ROBSON

Chapter One

Sacramento, California

The courthouse doors crashed open as I led my three sisters into the large foyer. I didn't mean to push so hard, but hell, I was mad and worried about being eaten. The cool spring breeze slapped at my back as I stepped inside, yet it did little to cool my temper or my nerves.

My nose scented the vampires before my eyes caught them emerging from the shadows. There were six of them, wearing dark suits, Ray-Bans, and obnoxious little grins. Two bolted the doors tight behind us, while the others frisked us for weapons.

I can't believe we we're in vampire court. So much for avoiding the perilous world of the supernatural.

Emme trembled beside me. She had every right to be scared. We were strong, but our combined abilities couldn't trump a roomful of bloodsucking beasts. "Celia," she whispered, her voice shaking. "Maybe we shouldn't have come."

Like we had a choice. "Just stay close to me, Emme." My

muscles tensed as the vampire's hands swept the length of my body and through my long curls. I didn't like him touching me, and neither did my inner tigress. My fingers itched with the need to protrude my claws.

When he finally released me, I stepped closer to Emme while I scanned the foyer for a possible escape route. Next to me, the vampire searching Taran got a little daring with his pat-down. But he was messing with the wrong sister.

"If you touch my ass one more time, fang boy, I swear to God I'll light you on fire." The vampire quickly removed his hands when a spark of blue flame ignited from Taran's fingertips.

Shayna, conversely, flashed a lively smile when the vampire searching her found her toothpicks. Her grin widened when he returned her seemingly harmless little sticks, unaware of how deadly they were in her hands. "Thanks, dude." She shoved the box back into the pocket of her slacks.

"They're clear." The guard grinned at Emme and licked his lips. "This way." He motioned her to follow. Emme cowered. Taran showed no fear and plowed ahead. She tossed her dark, wavy hair and strutted into the courtroom like the diva she was, wearing a tiny white mini dress that contrasted with her deep olive skin. I didn't fail to notice the guards' gazes glued to Taran's shapely figure. Nor did I miss when their incisors lengthened, ready to bite.

I urged Emme and Shayna forward. "Go. I'll watch your backs." I whipped around to snarl at the guards. The vampires' smiles faltered when they saw *my* fangs protrude. Like most beings, they probably didn't know what I was, but they seemed to recognize that I was potentially lethal, despite my petite frame.

I followed my sisters into the large courtroom. The place reminded me of a picture I'd seen of the Salem witch trials. Rows of dark wood pews lined the center aisle, and wide rustic planks comprised the floor. Unlike the photo I recalled, every window was boarded shut, and paintings of vampires hung on every inch of available wall space. One particular image epitomized the vampire stereotype perfectly. It showed a male vampire entwined with two naked women on a bed of roses and jewels. The women appeared completely enamored of the vampire, even while blood dripped from their necks.

The vampire spectators scrutinized us as we approached along the center aisle. Many had accessorized their expensive attire with diamond jewelry and watches that probably cost more than my car. Their glares told me they didn't appreciate my cotton T-shirt, peasant skirt, and flip-flops. I was twenty-five years old; it's not like I didn't know how to dress. But, hell, other fabrics and shoes were way more expensive to replace when I *changed* into my other form.

I spotted our accuser as we stalked our way to the front of the assembly. Even in a courtroom crammed with young and sexy vampires, Misha Aleksandr stood out. His tall, muscular frame filled his fitted suit, and his long blond hair brushed against his shoulders. Death, it seemed, looked damn good. Yet it wasn't his height or his wealth or even his striking features that captivated me. He possessed a fierce presence that commanded the room. Misha Aleksandr was a force to be reckoned with, but, strangely enough, so was I.

Misha had "requested" our presence in Sacramento after charging us with the murder of one of his family members. We had two choices: appear in court or be hunted for the rest of our lives. The whole situation sucked. We'd stayed hidden from the supernatural world for so long. Now not only had we been forced into the limelight, but we also faced the possibility of dying some twisted, Rob Zombie–inspired death.

Of course, God forbid that would make Taran shut her trap. She leaned in close to me. "Celia, how about I gather some magic-borne sunlight and fry these assholes?" she whispered in Spanish.

A few of the vampires behind us muttered and hissed, causing uproar among the rest. If they didn't like us before, they sure as hell hated us then.

Shayna laughed nervously, but maintained her perky demeanor. "I think some of them understand the lingo, dude."

I recognized Taran's desire to burn the vamps to blood and ash, but I didn't agree with it. Conjuring such power would leave her drained and vulnerable, easy prey for the master vampires, who would be immune to her sunlight. Besides, we were already in trouble with one master for killing his keep. We didn't need to be hunted by the entire leeching species.

The procession halted in a strangely wide-open area before a raised dais. There were no chairs or tables, nothing we could use as weapons against the judges or the angry mob amassed behind us.

My eyes focused on one of the boarded windows. The light honey-colored wood frame didn't match the darker boards. I guessed the last defendant had tried to escape. Judging from the claw marks running from beneath the frame to where I stood, he, she, or *it* hadn't made it.

I looked up from the deeply scratched floor to find Misha's intense gaze on me. We locked eyes, predator to predator, neither of us the type to back down. *You're trying to intimidate the wrong gal, pretty boy. I don't scare easily.*

Shayna slapped her hand over her face and shook her head, her long black ponytail waving behind her. "For Pete's sake, Celia, can't you be a little friendlier?" She flashed Misha a grin that made her blue eyes sparkle. "How's it going, dude?"

Shayna said "dude" a lot, ever since dating some idiot claiming to be a professional surfer. The term fit her sunny personality and eventually grew on us.

Misha didn't appear taken by her charm. He eyed her as if she'd asked him to make her a garlic pizza in the shape of a cross. I laughed; I couldn't help it. *Leave it to Shayna to try to befriend the guy who'll probably suck us dry by sundown.*

At the sound of my chuckle, Misha regarded me slowly.

His head tilted slightly as his full lips curved into a sensual smile. I would have preferred a vicious stare—I knew how to deal with those. For a moment, I thought he'd somehow made my clothes disappear and I was standing there like the bleeding hoochies in that awful painting.

The judges' sudden arrival gave me an excuse to glance away. There were four, each wearing a formal robe of red velvet with an elaborate powdered wig. They were probably several centuries old, but like all vampires, they didn't appear a day over thirty. Their splendor easily surpassed the beauty of any mere mortal. I guessed the whole "sucky, sucky, me love you all night" lifestyle paid off for them.

The judges regally assumed their places on the raised dais. Behind them hung a giant plasma screen, which appeared out of place in this century-old building. Did they plan to watch a movie while they decided how best to disembowel us?

A female judge motioned Misha forward with a Queen Elizabeth hand wave. A long, thick scar angled from the corner of her left jaw across her throat. Someone had tried to behead her. To scar a vampire like that, the culprit had likely used a gold blade reinforced with lethal magic. Apparently, even that blade hadn't been enough. I gathered she commanded the fang-fest Parliament, since her marble nameplate read, CHIEF JUSTICE ANTOINETTE MALIKA. Judge Malika didn't strike me as the warm and cuddly sort. Her lips were pursed into a tight line and her elongating fangs locked over her lower lip. I only hoped she'd snacked before her arrival.

At a nod from Judge Malika, Misha began. "Members of the High Court, I thank you for your audience." A Russian accent underscored his deep voice. "I hereby charge Celia, Taran, Shayna, and Emme Wird with the murder of my family member, David Geller."

"Wird? More like *Weird*," a vamp in the audience mumbled. The smaller vamp next to him adjusted his bow tie nervously when I snarled.

Oh, yeah, like we've never heard that before, jerk.

The sole male judge slapped a heavy leather-bound book on the long table and whipped out a feather quill. "Celia Wird. State your position."

Position?

I exchanged glances with my sisters; they didn't seem to know what Captain Pointy Teeth meant either. Taran shrugged. "Who gives a shit? Just say something."

I waved a hand. "Um. Registered nurse?"

Judging by his "please don't make me eat you before the proceedings" scowl, and the snickering behind us, I hadn't provided him with the appropriate response.

He enunciated every word carefully and slowly so as to not further confuse my obviously feeble and inferior mind. "Position in the supernatural world."

"We've tried to avoid your world." I gave Taran the evil eye. "For the most part. But if you must know, I'm a tigress."

"Weretigress," he said as he wrote.

"I'm not a *were*," I interjected defensively.

He huffed. "Can you *change* into a tigress or not?"

"Well, yes. But that doesn't make me a *were*."

The vamps behind us buzzed with feverish whispers while the judges' eyes narrowed suspiciously. Not knowing what we were made them nervous. A nervous vamp was a dangerous vamp. And the room was bursting with them.

"What I mean is, unlike a *were*, I can *change* parts of my body without turning into my beast completely." And unlike anything else on earth, I could also *shift*—disappear under and across solid ground and resurface unscathed. But they didn't need to know that little tidbit. Nor did they need to know I couldn't heal my injuries. If it weren't for Emme's unique ability to heal herself and others, my sisters and I would have died long ago.

"Fascinating," he said in a way that clearly meant I wasn't. The feather quill didn't come with an eraser. And the judge obviously didn't appreciate my making him mess up his book. He dipped his pen into his little inkwell and scribbled out what he'd just written before addressing Taran. "Taran Wird, position?"

"I can release magic into the forms of fire and lightning—"

"Very well, witch." The vamp scrawled.

"I'm not a witch, asshole."

The judge threw his plume on the table, agitated. Judge Malika fixed her frown on Taran. "What did you say?"

Nobody flashed a vixen grin better than Taran. "I said, 'I'm not a witch. Ass. Hole.'"

Emme whimpered, ready to hurl from the stress. Shayna giggled and threw an arm around Taran. "She's just kidding, dude!"

No. Taran didn't kid. Hell, she didn't even know any knock-knock jokes. She shrugged off Shayna, unwilling to back down. She wouldn't listen to Shayna. But she would listen to me.

"Just answer the question, Taran."

The muscles on Taran's jaw tightened, but she did as I asked. "I make fire, light—"

"Fire-breather." Captain Personality wrote quickly.

"I'm not a—"

He cut her off. "Shayna Wird?"

"Well, dude, I throw knives—"

"Knife thrower," he said, ready to get this little meet-and-greet over and done with.

Shayna did throw knives. That was true. She could also transform pieces of wood into razor-sharp weapons and manipulate alloys. All she needed was metal somewhere on her body and a little focus. For her safety, though, "knife thrower" seemed less threatening.

"And you, Emme Wird?"

"Um. Ah. I can move things with my mind—"

"Gypsy," the half-wit interpreted.

I supposed "telekinetic" was too big a word for this idiot. Then again, unlike typical telekinetics, Emme could do more than bend a few forks. I sighed. *Tigress, fire-breather, knife thrower, and Gypsy*. We sounded like the headliners for a freak show. All we needed was a bearded lady. I sighed. *That's what happens when you're the bizarre products of a back-fired curse.*

Misha glanced at us quickly before stepping forward once more. "I will present Mr. Hank Miller and Mr. Timothy Brown as witnesses—" Taran exhaled dramatically and twirled her hair like she was bored. Misha glared at her before finishing. "I do not doubt justice will be served."

Judge Zhahara Nadim, who resembled more of an Egyptian queen than someone who should be stuffed into a powdered wig, surprised me by leering at Misha like she wanted his head for a lawn ornament. I didn't know what he'd done to piss her off; yet knowing we weren't the only ones hated brought me a strange sense of comfort. She narrowed her eyes at Misha, like all predators do before they strike, and called forward someone named "Destiny." I didn't know Destiny, but I knew she was no vampire the moment she strutted onto the dais.

I tried to remain impassive. However, I really wanted to run away screaming. Short of sporting a few tails and some extra digits, Destiny was the freakiest thing I'd ever seen. Not only did she lack the allure all vampires possessed, but her fashion sense bordered on disastrous. She wore black patterned tights, white strappy sandals, and a hideous black-and-white polka-dot turtleneck. I guessed she sought to draw attention from her lime green zebra-print miniskirt. And, my God, her makeup was abominable. Black kohl outlined her bright fuchsia lips, and mint green shadow ringed her eyes.

"This is a perfect example of why I don't wear makeup," I told Taran.

Taran stepped forward with her hands on her hips. "How the hell is *she* a witness? I didn't see her at the club that night!

And Lord knows she would've stuck out."

Emme trembled beside me. "Taran, please don't get us killed!"

I gave my youngest sister's hand a squeeze. "Steady, Emme."

Judge Malika called Misha's two witnesses forward. "Mr. Miller and Mr. Brown, which of you gentlemen would like to go first?"

Both "gentlemen" took one gander at Destiny and scrambled away from her. It was never a good sign when something scared a vampire. Hank, the bigger of the two vamps, shoved Tim forward.

"You may begin," Judge Malika commanded. "Just concentrate on what you saw that night. Destiny?"

The four judges swiftly donned protective ear wear, like construction workers used, just as a guard flipped a switch next to the flat-screen. At first I thought the judges toyed with us. Even with heightened senses, how could they hear the testimony through those ridiculous ear guards? Before I could protest, Destiny enthusiastically approached Tim and grabbed his head. Tim's immediate bloodcurdling screams caused the rest of us to cover our ears. Every hair on my body stood at attention. What freaked me out was that he wasn't the one on trial.

Emme's fair freckled skin blanched so severely, I feared she'd pass out. Shayna stood frozen with her jaw open while Taran and I exchanged "oh, shit" glances. I was about to start the "let's get the hell out of here" ball rolling when images from Tim's mind appeared on the screen. I couldn't believe my eyes. Complete with sound effects, we relived the night of David's murder. Misha straightened when he saw David soar out of Taran's window in flames, but otherwise he did not react. Nor did Misha blink when what remained of David burst into ashes on our lawn. Still, I sensed his fury. The image moved to a close-up of Hank's shocked face and finished with the four of us scowling down at the blood and ash.

Destiny abruptly released the sobbing Tim, who collapsed on the floor. Mucus oozed from his nose and mouth. I didn't even know vamps were capable of such body fluids.

At last, Taran finally seemed to understand the deep shittiness of our situation. "Son of a bitch," she whispered.

Hank gawked at Tim before addressing the judges. "If it pleases the court, I swear on my honor I witnessed exactly what Tim Brown did about David Geller's murder. My version would be of no further benefit."

Malika shrugged indifferently. "Very well, you're excused." She turned toward us while Hank hurried back to his seat. "As you just saw, we have ways to expose the truth. Destiny is able to extract memories, but she cannot alter them. Likewise, during Destiny's time with you, you will be unable to change what you saw. You'll only review what has already come to pass."

I frowned. "How do we know you're telling us the truth?"

Malika peered down her nose at me. "What choice do you have? Now, which of you is first?"

Reader's Guide to the Magical World of the Weird

Girls Series

acute bloodlust A condition that occurs when a vampire goes too long without consuming blood. Increases the vampire's thirst to lethal levels. It is remedied by feeding the vampire.

Call The ability of one supernatural creature to reach out to another, through either thoughts or sounds. A vampire can pass his or her *call* by transferring a bit of magic into the receiving being's skin.

Change To transform from one being to another, typically from human to beast, and back again.

chronic bloodlust A condition caused by a curse placed on a vampire. It makes the vampire's thirst for blood insatiable and drives the vampire to insanity. The vampire grows in size from gluttony and assumes deformed features. There is no cure.

claim The method by which a werebeast consummates the union with his or her mate.

clan A group of werebeasts led by an Alpha. The types of clans differ depending on species. Werewolf clans are called "packs." Werelions belong to "prides."

Creatura The offspring of a demon lord and a werebeast.

dantem animam A soul giver. A rare being capable of returning a master vampire's soul. A master with a soul is more powerful than any other vampire in existence, as he or she is balancing life and death at once.

dark ones Creatures considered to be pure evil, such as shape-shifters or demons.

demon A creature residing in hell. Only the strongest demons may leave to stalk on earth, but their time is limited; the power of good compels them to return.

demon child The spawn of a demon lord and a mortal female. Demon children are of limited intelligence and rely predominantly on their predatory instincts.

demon lords (*demonkin*) The offspring of a witch mother and a demon. Powerful, cunning, and deadly. Unlike demons, whose time on earth is limited, demon lords may remain on earth indefinitely.

den A school where young werebeasts train and learn to fight in order to help protect the earth from mystical evil.

Elder One of the governors of a werebeast clan. Each clan is led by three Elders: an Alpha, a Beta, and an Omega. The Alpha is the supreme leader. The Beta is the second in command. The Omega settles disputes between them and has the ability to calm by releasing bits of his or her harmonized soul, or through a sense of humor muddled with magic. He possesses rare gifts and is often volatile, selfish, and of questionable loyalty.

force Emme Wird's ability to move objects with her mind.

gold The metallic element; it was cursed long ago and has damaging effects on werebeasts, vampires, and the dark ones. Supernatural creatures cannot hold gold without feeling the poisonous effects of the curse. A bullet dipped in gold will explode a supernatural creature's heart like a bomb. Gold against open skin has a searing effect.

grandmaster The master of a master vampire. Grandmasters are among the earth's most powerful creatures. Grandmasters can recognize whether the human he or she *turned* is a master upon creation. Grandmasters usually kill any master vampires they create to consume their power. Some choose to let the masters live until they become a threat, or until they've gained greater strength and therefore more consumable power.

Hag Hags, like witches, are born with their magic. They have a tendency for mischief and are as infamous for their instability as they are their power.

keep Beings a master vampire controls and is responsible for, such as those he or she has *turned* vampire, or a human he or she regularly feeds from. One master can acquire another's keep by destroying the master the keep belongs to.

Leader A pureblood werebeast in charge of delegating and planning attacks against the evils that threaten the earth.

Lesser witch Title given to a witch of weak power and who has not yet mastered control of her magic. Unlike their Superior counterparts, they aren't given talismans or staffs to amplify their magic because their control over their power is limited.

Lone A werebeast who doesn't belong to a clan, and therefore is not obligated to protect the earth from supernatural evil. Considered of lower class by those with clans.

master vampire A vampire with the ability to *turn* a human vampire. Upon their creation, masters are usually killed by their grandmaster for power. Masters are immune to fire and to sunlight born of magic, and typically carry tremendous power. Only a master or another lethal preternatural can kill a master vampire. If one master kills another, the surviving vampire acquires his or her power, wealth, and keep.

mate The being a werebeast will love and share a soul with for eternity.

Misericordia A plea for mercy in a duel.

moon sickness The werebeast equivalent of bloodlust. Brought on by a curse from a powerful enchantress. Causes excruciating pain. Attacks a werebeast's central nervous system, making the werebeast stronger and violent, and driving the werebeast to kill. No known cure exists.

mortem provocatio A fight to the death.

North American *Were* Council The governing body of *weres* in North America, led by a president and several council members.

potestatem bonum "The power of good." That which encloses the earth and keeps demons from remaining among the living.

Purebloods (aka *pures*) Werebeasts from generations of *were*-only family members. Considered royalty among werebeasts, they carry the responsibilities of their species. The mating between two purebloods is the only way to guarantee the conception of a *were* child.

rogue witch a witch without a coven. Must be accounted for as rogue witches tend to go one of two ways without a coven: dark or insane.

shape-shifter Evil, immortal creatures who can take any form. They are born witches, then spend years seeking innocents to sacrifice to a dark deity. When the deity deems the offerings sufficient, the witch casts a baneful spell to surrender his or her magic and humanity in exchange for immortality and the power of hell at their fingertips. Shape-shifters can command any form and are the deadliest and strongest of all mystical creatures.

Shift Celia's ability to break down her body into minute particles. Her gift allows her to travel beneath and across soil, concrete, and rock. Celia can also *shift* a limited number of beings. Disadvantages include not being able to breathe or see until she surfaces.

Skinwalkers Creatures spoken of in whispers and believed to be *weres* damned to hell for turning on their kind. A humanoid combination of animal and man that reeks of death, a *skinwalker* can manipulate the elements and subterranean arachnids. Considered impossible to kill.

solis natus magicae The proper term for sunlight born of magic, created by a wielder of spells. Considered "pure" light. Capable of destroying non-master vampires and demons. In large quantities may also kill shape-shifters. Renders the wielder helpless once fired.

Superior Witch A witch of tremendous power and magic who assumes a leadership role among the coven. Wears a talisman around her neck or carries staff with a precious stone at its center to help amplify her magic.

Surface Celia's ability to reemerge from a shift.

susceptor animae A being capable of taking one's soul, such as a vampire.

Trudhilde Radinka (aka *Destiny*) A female born once every century from the union of two witches who possesses rare talents and the aptitude to predict the future. Considered among the elite of the mystical world.

turn To transform a human into a werebeast or vampire. Werebeasts *turn* by piercing the heart of a human with their fangs and transferring a part of their essence. Vampires pierce through the skull and into the brain to transfer a taste of their magic. Werebeasts risk their lives during the *turning* process, as they are gifting a part of their souls. Should the transfer fail, both the werebeast and human die. Vampires risk nothing since they're not losing their souls, but rather taking another's and releasing it from the human's body.

vampire A being who consumes the blood of mortals to survive. Beautiful and alluring, vampires will never appear to age past thirty years. Vampires are immune to sunlight unless it is created by magic. They are also immune to objects of faith such as crucifixes. Vampires may be killed by the destruction of their hearts, decapitation, or fire.

Master vampires or vampires several centuries old must have both their hearts and heads removed or their bodies completely destroyed.

vampire clans Families of vampires led by master vampires. Masters can control, communicate, and punish their keep through mental telepathy.

velum A veil conjured by magic.

virtutem lucis "The power of light." The goodness found within each mortal. That which combats the darkness.

Warrior A werebeast possessing profound skill or fighting ability. Only the elite among *weres* are granted the title of Warrior. Warriors are duty-bound to protect their Leaders and their Leaders' mates at all costs.

werebeast A supernatural predator with the ability to *change* from human to beast. Werebeasts are considered the Guardians of the Earth against mystical evil. Werebeasts will achieve their first *change* within six months to a year following birth. The younger they are when they first *change,* the more powerful they will be. Werebeasts also possess the ability to heal their wounds. They can live until the first full moon following their one hundredth birthday. Werebeasts may be killed by destruction of their hearts, decapitation, or if their bodies are completely destroyed. The only time a *were* can partially

change is when he or she attempts to *turn* a human. A *turned* human will achieve his or her first *change* by the next full moon.

witch A being born with the power to wield magic. They worship the earth and nature. Pure witches will not take part in blood sacrifices. They cultivate the land to grow plants for their potions and use staffs and talismans to amplify their magic. To cross a witch is to feel the collective wrath of her coven.

witch fire Orange flames encased by magic, used to assassinate an enemy. Witch fire explodes like multiple grenades when the intended victim nears the spell. Flames will continue to burn until the target has been eliminated.

zombie Typically human bodies raised from the dead by a necromancer witch. It's illegal to raise or keep a zombie and is among the deadliest sins in the supernatural world. Their diet consists of other dead things such as roadkill and decaying animals.

Photo by Kate Gledhill of Kate Gledhill Photography

Cecy Robson (also writing as Rosalina San Tiago for the app Hooked) is an author of contemporary romance, young adult adventure, and award-winning urban fantasy. A double RITA® 2016 finalist for Once Pure and Once Kissed, and a published author of more than twenty novels, you can typically find Cecy on her laptop writing her stories or stumbling blindly in search of caffeine.

www.cecyrobson.com

Facebook.com/Cecy.Robson.Author

instagram.com/cecyrobsonauthor

twitter.com/cecyrobson

www.goodreads.com/goodreadscomCecyRobsonAuth
or

For exclusive information and more, join my Newsletter!

http://eepurl.com/4ASmj